D1382772

The Bequest

& Other Stories

The Bequest

& Other Stories

Jerry Wexler

Véhicule Press

Montréal, Canada

Acknowledgements

Some of these stories have appeared in *The Montreal Review, Jewish Dialogue, The Antigonish Review* and the anthology *Saturday Night at the Forum*. The 'Bequest' has been commissioned as a half-hour television drama by the National Film Board of Canada.

Published with the assistance of the Canada Council.

Cover painting by Philip Surrey. *107095*
Transparency of painting by Brian McNeil.
Colour separation by Synchrolith.
Photo of author by John Sleeman.
Book design by Simon Dardick.
Typesetting by Cusaset Inc.

Canadian Cataloguing in Publication Data

Wexler, Jerry, 1950-
    The bequest and other stories
ISBN: 0-919890-51-2

I. Title

PS8595.E95B47   1984   C813'.54   C84-090072-4
PR9199.3.W49B47   1984

Véhicule Press, P.O.B. 125, Place du Parc Station,
Montréal, Québec, Canada   H2W 2M9

Printed in Canada.

Contents

For my parents
&
for Mary Lee and Jonah

Jerry Wexler's Quiet City Nights

My wife and I had believed for a long time that we were almost the only people who had regularly patronized the tiny restaurant *Tony du Sud*, and now we find that Jerry Wexler has fixed the look, the colour and atmosphere, the sound, the patterns of movement in that very small space, as skilfully and finally as a great photographer, a Cartier-Bresson, a Sam Tata. I can't remember how I happened to stumble on the place. I think I had a dinner date with somebody who lived near the corner of Fairmount and Clark—it may have been some guy from the CBC—and he suggested that we dine there. It was a step into the world of Wexler.

The sense of life being lived with a peculiar infinitesimal purposefulness, like that of sympathetic and very intelligent insects, which pervades Jerry Wexler's work, cannot have been more wholly realised than in *Tony du Sud*, model for the restaurant so exquisitely fixed in the opening pages of the beautiful story, "Your Eighteenth Birthday was a Long Time Ago." I don't think the place can ever have held more than, say, two dozen diners at once, and that under crowded conditions. There were a couple of tables to either side of the entrance, maybe three stools at the serving bar, next the cash register, and a recess or alcove to the right of the room behind the cash desk, in all space for limited action with elbows, knife and fork. You could bring your own wine, or drink the home-made wine of the house from mugs, if I remember rightly. I distinctly recall the colour of Tony's home-made vintage; it was not the colour of any other growth known to me. It looked like cream soda.

I knew that the proprietor had prospered in another location after the tiny hole-in-the-wall had closed, but for one reason or another, I never went looking for the new place on St. Lawrence.

11

But Jerry did. That's my point. One man will see a story possibility where another won't, and the story possibilities that you recognise are the ones that in the end constitute your special art. The story about Tony's two restaurants and the time that separates them is the essential Wexler narrative. It is about a single person, with one other person, his lover, positioned as a nearby satellite unable to move right into his space. It is a city story. It takes place mostly at night. It relies for its central effect on accurate poised evocation of scene. It has clear analogies with musical procedures, especially those of instrumentation. It moves towards one of the profound human affirmations, when its tone becomes that of ethical or religious meditation:

> Hyman lay back and in a moment returned to this semi-awake state that served as a conduit for his prayers. "And for sleep there is hope too," he thought. "Yes, and there are dreams that don't die in the morning but that well through the body like a shudder on a vacant street. And sleep really is just a respite between dreams, for all is possible and there really are realms of adventure. Perhaps," he thought. "Of course," he answered. "Of course there is no fear. And I have no fear. The day will always be brave. And sleep...and sleep will always welcome our night."
> (YOUR EIGHTEENTH BIRTHDAY WAS A LONG TIME AGO)

The stories regularly move from minute observation of scene towards states of mind that suggest the tone of the Judaeo-Christian Scriptures, as in the closing lines of "The Bequest."

> We sat again, without speaking, in the dark living-room. I could not tell if she had truly meant what she said, or had just said it to agree with me, make me feel better.
> That night Claire stayed with me. It was the first time in two years. I suppose it was her way of acknowledging the great sadness that had come upon me. The silence was only broken at two in the morning by an upstairs neighbour calling to tell me that a pipe had broken and would I call a plumber immediately.

There you go, from "the great sadness that had come upon me," the language of the prophets, to "would I call a plumber immediately," more the language of Woody Allen. This in the middle of the night, with an inscrutable and uncomprehending lover (named Claire) at one's side. That's the Jerry Wexler trip. Or once again:

> As I touched him he opened his eyes and slightly turned his head to look at me. "Everything's going to be all right, Dad," I said. "Don't worry, everything's going to be all right."
>
> (LAMENT FOR A SON)

Well of course that's what we all want, and hope for. The affirmation reminds me of some of the great speeches on the subject delivered by characters in the plays of Chekhov. Maybe everything isn't going to be all right. Probably it isn't. But we hope it is.

All of Wexler's stories attempt to fix and transmit a special and particular mode of feeling, not necessarily a 'good' or 'bad' feeling, but always a pervasive, spreading, feeling/tone, which by the end of the story has become almost oppressively moving. This is where these texts are like musical scores. They try to make their readers *feel* in highly specific terms. They remind you of Debussy in the felicity of their choice of exposed voices, and sometimes of the American disciples of Debussy and Stravinsky taught by Nadia Boulanger. I think of the city music of Sessions, Kennan, Aaron Copland, David Diamond, when I read Wexler: the same evocation of solitude at night amidst sleeping millions.

The long-nosed ladies and gents who teach Canadian literature in the solemn academies never tire of telling us in their conventional wisdom that our writing is about small-town or country or wilderness life in an isolated and menaced situation, faced by the immense wilderness. Callaghan? MacLennan? Davies? This hasn't been so for fifty years. if it ever was so in any sense. Gallant, Blaise, Metcalf, Rooke, Munro, these aren't the frightened foot soldiers of Old Fort Henry or suicidal farmers with shit on their boots. They are people who confront the writing of the world on the great world's terms, and so is Jerry Wexler, intrinsically and triumphantly a writer about hope and holiness—the holiness celebrated by the Psalmist—in the city, who writes with an immense awareness of his predecessors in the art. A fully literate man, not a naif, not a savage, noble or ignoble, an artist.

They sure do keep coming along, don't they? The artists. They don't back off and they don't quit, and though for a while in the seventies it looked like there was an interruption in the proces-

13

sion, we can now see that the ranks are filling up again. Doug Glover, Peter Behrens, Guy Vanderhaeghe, and on the specifically Montréal scene at least four important writers who are in no sense a school, who write in very different ways and take very different points of departure, but who are all living here in the nineteen-eighties, writing superbly about four separate sets of story posibilities. Terence Byrnes, Lorris Elliott, Mel Dagg, Jerry Wexler. I don't doubt that there are others coming along right behind them, perhaps Miriam Packer or Maryse Warda. The procession hasn't ended, it's just getting started, and here comes Jerry Wexler at its head. Start reading now.

Hugh Hood
Monteal, 1983

The Bequest

IT WAS SARAH who told me about the flat on Esplanade. She had seen the "for rent" sign tacked to the door and knowing I was looking for a place in the neighbourhood, had called me. It was nice of her. It's good to have friends, I suppose.

At that time I was living with my younger brother in a very old flat on Duluth St. near Hotel de Ville, across from the Portuguese Fish Market. It was not really a suitable place for me, but at the time I moved there six months before it seemed like the best option. Previously, I had lived with my wife for four years in an apartment in lower Westmount. It was a pleasant apartment in a pleasant neighbourhood. It was also a dull neighbourhood. No bars, few shops, hardly any restaurants. But one can live without any of these things when one is in love and is content to sit at home in an armchair, reading a book, knowing that someone is around to share your space. I was a private person. We were a private couple. A nice Westmount way to be.

But it wasn't such a nice way to be after three years. The fights began between us, the insinuations, the mistrust, the infidelities. I still can't understand why, completely. Our backgrounds must have had something to do with it. She was English, Anglo-Saxon. Her father was a doctor and a chief medical consultant for a large insurance company. She was a champion skier, spent her summers in the family country house in New Brunswick. I was Jewish, born and raised on St. Urbain St., at that time the Jewish working class neighbourhood in Montreal. My father was a pedlar on St. Lawrence Boulevard, in the immigrant shopping district. He bought cheap and sold cheap, carrying goods around in the trunk of his old car. As a child I had spent my summers help-

17

ing him, travelling in the uncomfortably hot car, carting parcels in and out of stores. My free time was spent on the street itself, sitting on stoops on summer evenings with my friends, learning about sex, or arguing about how the Canadiens would do in the next hockey season.

But I had, in a way, grown out of this world, or at least apart from it. I had gone on to university to study Shakespeare and Milton, had written a thesis on Spenser's *Faerie Queene*, and was now a lecturer in a university. My closest acquaintances were other professors with Phds from Oxford and the University of Toronto. When we met each other for dinner it was always "please pass the roast beef"—never the "gimmee" of my youth. Claire was content with her world, who she was and what she belonged to. My consciousness lay in more than one camp, and I always had a hidden, but nevertheless deep-felt, doubt about where in fact I did belong.

And I was also given to saying silly things which I regretted soon after. Perhaps it was my East European heritage that made me more volatile. I used to say that my collective unconscious lay on the steppes of the Ukraine, in villages where the huts had mud floors and women screamed at their children and husbands, while her collective unconscious lay in a tea room on the Isle of Wight. I was too tempermental and in Claire's shadow began to feel like a mensch who had never made it. Claire was different. For a long time I had felt, as extreme as it may sound, that she was perfect. I admired everything about her—her clarity and honesty and sureness about herself—and for three years of our marriage, despite these variances in our characters, we did fit well together and allowed our differences to complement each other.

But the fourth year was hard. Her family never really accepted me. I desperately wanted my family to accept Claire, but Claire never really tried for acceptance. She became more private, withdrawn, wanted more time to herself, and I hung on and didn't really give her the room she said she needed. I found it difficult because I still loved her. Anyway, it is no longer important who slapped who in the face, who broke the typewriter by throwing it on the floor, who lay up all night, crying. It happened and that is all that is important. We were both sad, but it had happened. The apartment was hers originally and I offered to be the one to move.

I decided to, in a sense, return to my roots, to move back to a neighbourhood where I might feel comfortable. I wanted to move back to the area around St. Urbain St. and live with the Greek and Portuguese immigrants who now populated this place where dirty children played hockey in the streets, and one could eat souvlaki at two in the morning. I would even be close to the Hassidim who lived on Waverly St. They, of course, would not acknowledge me, but they could form a section of this new world of mine. I still remember myself, as a child, standing outside their study halls at night and seeing the hundreds of books that lined the walls of their front rooms. Their studies were bathed in a warm glow and every so often I would catch a glimpse of one of the black-clad men sitting at a table, rocking back and forth in the ecstasy of learning.

I had been gone a long time. I was now thirty-two and had lived in my world of suburban students and Westmount complacency for too long. It was time for a change, to perhaps even become something of a new person, if such a thing is truly possible.

The flat that Sarah found seemed to be everything that I had hoped for. I closed my eyes to the fact that it was dark, the walls were bulging and plaster was peeling from the ceilings. The flat was heated by an oil stove that sat in the middle of the house, and I remember from my youth that they were smelly and messy affairs. But none of that mattered to me at this point. What I saw before me was a second floor flat with a gingerbread porch. Five rooms to grow in, to fill with warm furniture, to hang plants in by the windows, to fill with books and music and new friends.

The young French couple who let me view the apartment gave me the phone number of the landlady, warning me that she was a vile person. But I was still blind to anything negative related to the flat. It felt like my space and that was all that mattered.

I noticed that the landlady had an unusual name, Feldhanner. Obviously Jewish. I could handle her, I thought. But I would have to act quickly. These flats, despite their often decrepit condition, were in great demand. I called her from the flat while the French couple looked on.

Someone answered "Hello" at the other end of the line. It was just one word but I could already visualize the bearer of that voice. She must be at least sixty. Probably had lived in that house many years ago. Now she did not care for the house at all but hung on to it as a source of income. I would have to act with tact. But I knew her type. The trick would be to sign the lease first and argue about the condition of the flat later.

"Mrs. Feldhanner, my name is Ben, Ben Nudleman. I have viewed your flat on Esplanade and find it quite suitable. I would like to make arrangements to rent it." The trick was to let her know I was Jewish and at the same time sound educated. Ten points in my favor, at least.

"Well listen, Mr. Nudleman, this is a very fine flat and I am very particular about who lives there." Her voice had a heavy East European accent with its accompanying high pitched whine. She was probably, as they would say in the Yiddish vernacular, a yenta.

"Well, I am a very reliable person, Mrs. Feldhanner. I'm sure you won't have any trouble with me."

"What kind of work do you do Mr. Nudleman? I only want respectable tenants, you understand."

At this point I was almost smirking. I found her interrogation truly amusing. We were playing a game and I was sure I would win.

Oh, I'm very respectable, I replied. "I teach English at a university here in Montreal. I work every day." Now she knew that I had a full-time job and was a college teacher to boot. Another ten points at least.

"Tell me," she said, "do you come from Montreal?"

"I do," I replied.

"So you have family here?"

"Oh yes," I said. She was obviously checking to see if she would have recourse to someone if I did not pay my rent. I could rack up another ten points.

"I see, I see." Her voice began to trail off. I was sure she had already settled on letting me have the place.

"Well, listen, Mr. Nudleman. You know I have to raise the

rent. I will have to charge two hundred and fifty dollars a month."
The young French couple had told me they were paying one
hundred and seventy dollars a month. She was asking an exorbi-
tant increase. But I couldn't lose my cool now.

"That is a bit more than I intended to pay but I am sure we
can come to an arrangement. When can we meet?"

I had probably caught her off guard. I heard her utter an
elongated, almost timid, "well" followed by thirty seconds of
silence. She was sizing up the situation.

"Come this afternoon. 5620 Côte des Neiges, Apartment 11.
But only come after three because I take my walk before then."
Then she hung up. There was no good-bye.

I hung up the receiver, smiling to myself. "You didn't do too
badly, old boy," I thought. Match and Game.

I returned to my brother's to put on some clean clothes. I
decided to wear my tweed sports jacket. Claire had always said I
looked like a professor in it. Not a bad recommendation. I was
sure to look respectable to Mrs. Feldhanner.

I arrived at her apartment at three-thirty. She lived in a post-
war apartment building in the Côte des Neiges district of Montreal. It was an architecturally nondescript district where the
Jewish population had migrated to in the fifties. I had always
found it to be a sad area, in many ways. Many of the people who
lived there were old and retired. But they had not grown old
gracefully. They were beset by the ills of the twentieth century and
their culture. Most of the people were overweight, having lived on
a diet of sour cream and fatty meats. They had no spring in their
walk but rather were stooped and wrinkled and walked with a
resigned shuffle. The women were, in a way, the most pathetic.
The men generally made no effort to cover up what they were.
They usually hung around the shopping centres and gossipped
with one another in their suits and baggy, cuffed pants. But the
women so often covered their age and decay with layers of make-
up. They wore printed skirts, which hugged their fat haunches
and walked with a slow gait, not far removed from a waddle.

Many years before, in my student days, I had worked on a

farm in Ireland. I remember how strong and hardy the old people were who lived on the farms and in the small villages. At the age of seventy-five they could still raise fifty pounds of hay over their heads with a pitchfork and work eight hours a day in the fields. Their faces were creased, but not with lines of decay. They were lines etched by years of standing in blowing winds and evening mists and grasping the earth in slow, hard labour.

When I returned to Montreal I felt sad for these older Jewish people, the golden-agers as they called them, standing idly in shopping centres and shuffling slowly and awkwardly down city streets.

Mrs. Feldhanner answered the doorbell. She looked about sixty.

She was wearing the regulation make-up, mostly rouge covering full cheeks, as well as the floral patterned skirt. A pair of horn-rimmed glasses, inlaid with rhinestones, hung on a chain from her neck.

"Mrs. Feldhanner."

"Yes."

"I'm Ben Nudleman." I offered her my hand and she shook it lightly, suspiciously.

"Come in, Mr. Nudleman." We sat down in her living room.

When we seemed to be comfortable she said, "Yes, Mr. Nudleman. Now I have thought about you renting the flat. You want it for yourself, I assume."

I nodded.

"Yes, well you see, I have had bad experiences with bachelors. They throw wild parties and don't keep the apartment in good repair. The rent on the flat was going to be two hundred and fifty dollars but I will have to charge you two hundred and eighty dollars a month."

I was stunned. Her logic astounded me. She was obviously a miser and was prepared to invent any reason to take advantage of someone. Here I was, dressed in my best clothes, trying to act in an erudite manner, and I was forced to deal with someone who was off her rocker. I was close to losing my cool and knew I would have to watch myself. I didn't want to blow it.

"Mrs. Feldhanner," I replied, "I really fail to see your logic. I am a very quiet, tidy person, and assure you I will cause no damage to the apartment." My remarks about damage seemed so ironic as I visualized the apartment and remembered the poor repair that it was already in.

"Well, Mr. Nudleman," she answered, "I think my offer is very logical and fair."

I was getting frustrated. I wanted the flat but didn't want to be cheated.

"Tell me, Mrs. Feldhanner. If a family with a small child asked to rent the flat, would you also charge them more? Or if a young couple wanted the flat, would you charge them more, because two people cause more wear on an apartment than one person?"

"Mr. Nudleman, that has nothing to do with us. I have offered you my terms."

I was stuck. She was crazy. But I still wanted the flat. It had the right feel for me. Mrs Feldhanner aside, I felt that moving into that place would probably be the best thing I could do for myself at that stage of my life. I had to think fast. The money itself wasn't important. I could easily afford the extra thirty dollars a month. But it was, as they say, the principle of the thing. I just didn't want to be dictated to by a crazy old lady. I decided to agree to her terms and then afterwards find some sort of legal loophole to either reduce the rent, or get vengeance on her in some other way. Giving in temporarily at least, seemed like the only way of getting the place.

"All right," I said, "we might as well sign the lease."

She already had two of the new government leases prepared. She filled in the necessary information in a jagged, scratchy handwriting. It was tense writing, as tense as she was. Then it was over. I left her apartment in a somewhat elated mood, despite the unpleasant bargaining. I had my new home at last.

And it did become my home. I filled it with books, the typewriter (now repaired), old furniture and rugs. I made friends

23

with my neighbours. There was a whole community on the street—students, artists, musicians. A young lady next door who was a design student at a theatre school volunteered to sew curtains. My upstairs neighbour was an experimental photographer and I carried on conversations with him through the skylight that ran through the house. That summer I often sat on my porch or on my steps drinking tea. There was constant activity on the streets—people washing their cars, shopping, congregating in groups for impromptu conversations. On Sundays Park Avenue would be filled with Greek and Portuguese families dressed in their finest clothes. I don't suppose they were going anywhere in particular. They were just out for a promenade. And my brother with whom I had lived before would often walk over to visit me. The strain between us evaporated and we would often sit around my large pine table in the kitchen and talk about life and politics and occasionally those politics of the heart we sometimes call love.

The flat became a comfortable home, an environment that suited me, where I could feel at ease. Even Claire began to visit me. Not often, perhaps every three weeks, but it was a sign that she did not feel as distant from me as before. Time had helped patch over bad feelings. I think she may have even looked on visiting me as a type of adventure. Visiting my neighbourhood, for her, must have been a bit like visiting a foreign country, even an exotic country. It was a great excursion and I enjoyed sharing the adventure with her.

I had made a comfortable home for myself. But I could not hide for too long from the fact that my home was also an old decaying house. During the winter it smelled of oil from the heater that stood in the centre of the house. All the plaster in the bathroom was either cracked or peeling, and the bathtub tap ran incessantly.

Mrs. Feldhanner, of course, had no inclination at all to do my repairs. She would call me if my rent cheque had not arrived by the third of the month, but would always deny any responsibility or necessity to maintain the house. Problems that arose with the house were of my own doing. It was all blamed on me when the double windows blew out of their rotten frames, when the banister to the front stairs collapsed and the third floor balcony began to sag dangerously. I would argue with her on the phone to the point of becoming distraught about repairs that had to be done. She would shriek back at me, accuse me of being an evil person who should never have rented the flat in the first place if I was not satisfied with its condition. During particularly heated moments she would yell at me in Yiddish. I would yell back that I didn't speak Yiddish and that she shouldn't take it for granted that I did. There would always follow a long pause after that retort. Then she would say, "That's all I have to say," and would hang up. I often wondered what she was thinking during that long pause.

Montreal had one of its coldest spells in history during the February of the second year I lived in the flat. The temperature hovered between minus twenty and minus thirty degrees Celsius for almost the whole month. My pipes froze as they did in almost every house on the street. Plumbers' trucks were a regular sight in front of neighbours' homes. I knew Mrs. Feldhanner would not want to take responsibility for paying a plumber to unfreeze the pipes but I had to call her anyway. I shuddered to think of the fight that would ensue, but I was still conscious of principle. I would not give up the rights due to me as a tenant.

"Hello, Mrs. Feldhanner."

"Yes?"

"This is Ben here." I no longer used my second name in identifying myself to her. People who regularly scream at each other have no need to be officious. "The pipes are frozen in my house, Mrs. Feldhanner."

She was silent. She knew what was coming and was probably preparing herself.

"O.K., Mrs. Feldhanner. The pipes are frozen and it is your responsibility to call a plumber to unfreeze them. If you do not call a plumber immediately I will call one of my own choosing and deduct his fee from my rent."

Then she spoke. She was agitated. She was not shouting yet,

but her voice had a nervous, intense tone to it.

"Very nice, Mr. Nudleman," she said. "What are you trying to do, frighten me? Well you don't frighten me at all. Why did you rent the apartment if you didn't like the plumbing? You live there, it is your responsibility, not mine."

It was anger time. I could not remain calm in the face of her unreasonableness.

"Listen, you stupid lady," I said to her, "you own the house, you have to maintain it. If you don't call a plumber immediately, I will call one myself. I don't want to argue about it."

"I don't want to argue either, Mr. Nudleman," she replied. "Why do you bother me with all your complaints? I have so many expenses with that miserable house. "I've spent too much money on it already."

Her reply infuriated me. "That's a lie," I shouted back. "You haven't fixed a thing in this house for years. Your only expense is the municipal tax and that's nothing on a house like this. Listen to yourself, Mrs. Feldhanner, listen how you lie to other people."

"Don't you lecture me, Mr. Nudleman. I'm a lot older than you. Don't you tell me what to do."

I was silent for a moment. I was still agitated. But when I spoke again it was with a more assured, almost superior tone.

"Do you know what you are, Mrs. Feldhanner? You are an evil person. Really."

She shouted back immediately, "And don't you give me no business about being a bad person."

But I continued and this time my voice rose again.

"You are evil." I spoke quickly now. I didn't want to give her room to interrupt. "And I'll tell you why. Because you are a miser and a cheat and a liar. Don't you realize what kind of person you are? Don't you realize that the other tenants in this building hate you and that I'm the only person who will even talk to you? But what's worse, Mrs. Feldhanner, what's worse, is that other people see you are a Jew and they think that all Jews are like you. You hurt your own people. Don't you realize any of that?"

"What do you know about being a Jew, Mr. Nudleman? Tell me, when was the last time you were in a synagogue? Even your wife wasn't Jewish. I know, I once saw her coming out of your

26

house, last summer. I could tell just by looking at her. I even spoke to her."

I was surprised that she had met Claire. It must have been a strange sight. The old wretch and the prim, young lady standing on the street outside the house. But what amazed me more was her whole train of argument. She had completely missed the point of everything I had said. I was frustrated. How could I argue with her, reason with her? I switched the topic back to the frozen pipes. I had hoped to shame her, to make her realize what kind of person she really was. But it was just too much work and at this point I lacked the patience.

"My wife has nothing to do with any of this," I said. "I just want my pipes fixed. If you don't call a plumber I am going to hire my own and deduct his fee from my rent."

"You don't threaten me, Mr. Nudleman. You don't threaten me at all. I'll send back your cheque if it isn't for the full amount."

"Send it back if you want. I won't send you another." At that point I hung up, before she had time to do so herself.

I did call my own plumber and I did deduct his fee of forty-two dollars from the rent. My cheque to Mrs. Feldhanner came back three days later. I was determined not to send her another one.

Mrs. Feldhanner called me several times in the next two weeks demanding full payment. She threatened law suits, sending the police, evicting me. But I held fast. It was this old matter of principle. But I did notice a great change coming over her by the third week of this standoff. Her voice became less agressive, less angry. She began to speak more softly, almost timidly. She would almost politely, or as politely as she could, request that I send her a new cheque. She was genuinely afraid that I would not send her one. At times she sounded almost pleading and for the first time I began to see her not as an angry, vocal adversary but as an old lady, alone and helpless in a frightening world which she did not quite understand. But I held fast. The memories of the arguments, the fights, the shouting were still too strong. Perhaps I was in reality punishing her for all these. Perhaps it was now my turn to harm.

It was towards the end of this period that Claire came to visit. It was a Saturday afternoon and I was at my desk correcting term papers. It was cold outside, but the house was comfortable and warm inside, a sort of midwinter sanctuary. I had covered all the windows with plastic sheeting and that had helped cut out drafts that seeped through the rotten window frames. When Claire took off her coat I saw she wearing a man's grey suit. It was an unusual outfit but it suited her well. All her carefully chosen clothes suited her, made her look attractive.

We had tea in the kitchen, at my pine table. I offered her some baklava that I had bought at the Greek bakery around the corner. She had never tasted that pastry made from nuts and layers of flaky dough covered in honey syrup. She enjoyed it. Afterwards we talked for awhile about work, how we were managing on our own, if the Westmount flat had changed much. We carefully skirted matters of other love affairs. I didn't want to know and she felt she shouldn't tell me, for fear probably of hurting me. But I was pretty sure she had had other affairs and was probably having one now. I could sense it. But I wouldn't discuss it.

The conversation drifted around to Mrs. Feldhanner and my problems with the house.

"You shouldn't get so worked up about it," she said.

"I know I shouldn't," I replied. "But I just can't help it. She irritates me so much. She yells into the phone, she lies and cheats, has no sense of fairness. She refuses to fix anything. She's probably praying for the building to burn down so she can collect the insurance."

"So you should be more cool with her. Treat her like more of a human being."

"That just it. That's what bothers me so much. She's such a bad specimen of humanity. It depresses me to think that there are actually people like her around."

"Come on, Ben," answered Claire. "What's this business about specimen of humanity? She's human, like everyone else, with strengths and weaknesses, like anyone."

I was silent for a moment. Claire was rationalizing something that I was reacting to in a purely emotional way. She was very good at that. She had done that all through our marriage and

I found it difficult to argue with her because her coolness made my emotion seem silly, almost childish.

"She doesn't have any children, you know," said Claire.

Her remark struck me by surprise.

"How do you know that?" I asked.

"Oh, I've spoken to her."

I remembered Mrs. Feldhanner telling me that they had met last summer. The vision came to me again of the young lady standing poised and assured talking to the painted old Jewish lady. What would they have had to talk about?

"So, what does whether or not she has children have to do with anything?" I asked.

"Oh, I think it has to do with a lot of things. Don't you see it?" Claire spoke as if I was guilty of being unaware of something very obvious that I should have realized a long time ago. She was good at that too.

I was silent for a moment. Then I turned to her.

"Look, I know what you're getting at," I said. "But tell me something. Why are you laying this mother trip on me anyway? You're the one who was always uncomfortable around my family. You never even made an effort to get to know my own mother, to find out what this whole Jewish mother business was about anyway."

"Oh, I understood, Ben. I understood a lot." She spoke in a low voice but looked directly at me as she spoke. Then she bowed her head slightly.

I was puzzled. Our conversation was now becoming very quiet, and intense. Claire and I were exploring each other in a way that we hadn't done before.

"What else did you talk about to Mrs. Feldhanner that day, when you met her?" I asked. I was curious. The image of the two of them standing before the house came to me again.

"Oh, not much," said Claire. We'll talk about it another time if you want. Anyway, I should be going now. I'll see you soon."

She rose from the table, put on her winter coat and left. It seemed as though she was purposely avoiding getting further involved in any discussion about her life, my life, and that of Mrs. Feldhanner which had become so strangely intertwined.

I watched from my window as she crossed the silent street with its high snow banks piled on either side. She walked, not quite sure footed in the deep snow, the hood off exposing her curly brown hair, and as I looked on I could not help but remark to myself how handsome a woman she still appeared to be.

Three days later Mrs. Feldhanner called me. It was now the twenty-fifth of the month. I had still not sent her a cheque.

"Mr. Nudleman."

"Yes."

I noticed that her voice was much weaker. It lacked the strength, the aggression that had characterized it before.

"Mr. Nudleman, please," she said feebly, "I don't have the strength for this business. I know it's a very old house and maybe not everything works right, but I can't keep fixing it all. It's just too much. I keep trying to sell the house but nobody wants to buy it." Then, almost as an aside she said, "Someone else should find out how much trouble it is these days to be a proprietor." She finished by saying, "Please be a nice person and send me the money you owe me."

Because she had sounded so weak, and almost rational, I replied in a fairly calm, reasoning voice. For once I was not afraid of being interrupted before I finished my sentence.

"Mrs. Feldhanner, it really isn't fair for me to send you all the money. Everybody knows that frozen pipes are the responsibility of the landlord."

"Listen, Mr. Nudleman. I don't have the strength any more. Please, do what's right. Good-bye."

She hung up. It was the first time she had ever said good-bye.

I waited a couple of days. I was still legally right, I knew that, but somehow this matter of principle didn't matter any more. I thought of Claire, and our conversation, and I thought of Mrs. Feldhanner's weak defeated voice. I suppose, in a way, I had won. In this battle of wills it seemed that she had lost and was now subservient to me. But I didn't feel like much of a victor. All I had done was weaken an old lady. Perhaps that is what Claire realized was happening, and was what she hinted at in that conversation.

She did understand a lot, perhaps more than me. All of a sudden Claire seemed very wise; everybody seemed very wise, and I felt very foolish. The next day I sent Mrs. Feldhanner a cheque for the full amount.

I seldom spoke to Mrs. Feldhanner in the succeeding months. I began to assume more responsibility for the flat myself. I bought the *Reader's Digest* book of home repairs and instead of demanding that Mrs. Feldhanner fix things that were broken, I began to repair them myself. I plastered a couple of ceilings, replaced broken faucets, even sanded and varnished the living room floor. Claire continued to visit. There was still a certain distance between us, a certain hesitancy, but the gap was not as wide as before. It seemed as though she was looking at me as a different type of person, as if she understood more about me. My new living room with sanded floors and recently painted white walls seemed to complement our new relationship. That was where we would sit while we drank our afternoon tea, listened to music, talked or sat in silence. Sometimes I would just stare at her and a minute or more would often pass before she became self-conscious and turned away.

The lawyer's letter came in mid-August. It was from the firm of Bernstein, Bernstein, Solomon and Abbott. I had never received a lawyer's letter before. I stared at the unopened envelope for several moments. It must have something to do with Mrs. Feldhanner, I thought. Possibly an eviction notice. The old bitch must be up to her tricks again, and after all the work I had done on the flat at my own expense. The anger that had dissipated in the past few months began to well up again. I opened the letter, the mental picket fences and armaments already in position. The letter read:

> Dear Mr. Nudleman;
> We regret to inform you that the proprietor of your residence, Mrs. Bella Feldhanner, passed away on the first of August. As you have been entered as a beneficiary in her will we suggest that

you make an appointment to visit us at your earliest convenience.

Sincerely,
Simon Bernstein, Advocat

The anger disappeared immediately. Her death was a surprise, of course. She was my landlady, someone to fight with, or somewhat peacefully co-exist with at a far distance. But the idea of her dying had never really occurred to me and I was unsure exactly how to react—whether to feel sorrow. . . or relief.

It was Mr. Bernstein Jr. who I saw at the law office. He seemed to be about thirty and was quite polite, and official.

"Yes, Mr. Nudleman. Have a seat. Cigarette? That's all right, I intend to kick the habit myself. Well, down to business. As you know, Mrs. Feldhanner appointed our firm as executors of her will. You may also know that in reality her estate was quite small. She had donated her household furniture to various charities. Her only major asset was her building on Esplanade, which she has left you."

So that was it. She had left me the building. But why this strange bequest? And why me?

"What about other members of her family?" I asked

"As far as we know she had no blood relatives in Montreal, or anywhere for that matter. I believe she lost her family during the war. There shouldn't be any problem in finalizing the transfer of property."

I leaned forward in my seat. I was trying to comprehend these strange events that were now occurring.

"But I can't understand why she would possibly want to leave the property to me," I said. "I was just her tenant and we never got along very well, anyway."

Young Mr. Bernstein relaxed his pose and sat back in his swivel-rocker chair.

"Well, Mr. Nudleman. I can't answer that at all. We only serve as executors of her will."

"Do you have any idea how much the house is worth?" I asked.

"I know that the last city evaluation assessed it at eighteen

32

thousand dollars. But as you probably know the building is not in very good condition. The city has been threatening for some time to condemn it. Apparently the electrical wiring dates back to 1920. You will now be responsible for all these matters, of course."

Young Mr. Bernstein grimaced slightly, awkwardly. It was a type of grimace that said, "Sorry, buddy, that's the way things are, you know."

Great, I thought to myself. Now I have a condemned building on my hands. I began to see images of the house. The peeling plaster, rotten windows and sagging balconies. All of this was now mine. Images of Mrs. Feldhanner also appeared in my mind. They were images that blended the two Mrs. Feldhanners that I knew—the loud, aggressive proprietor and timid, weak old lady.

My silent observations were broken by Mr. Bernstein's voice: "Well, Mr. Nudleman, I have a busy schedule today and other clients are waiting. If you'd like to come by next week, say on Wednesday, I'll have the proper documents for transferring the property drawn up for your signature."

"All right," I said. I rose and opened his office door, still caught up in my images of the past. Just before I left I turned and found myself asking him, "By the way, what did she die of?"

"Oh, I thought you knew," he said. "It was cancer. She's had it for at least four years, knew she was dying all along. It's amazing that she held on so long."

"Oh," I said. Then I left.

Two days later Claire came to visit. It was night. I had invited her. We sat in the newly refurbished living room on the white rug. The lights were off. I had been very silent the past two days since leaving the lawyer's office and darkness suited my mood. Gradually, our eyes adjusted and we could discern each other reasonably well. Claire must have realized that I was troubled. Perhaps that is why she waited patiently, not breaking the silence.

"I can't understand it," I finally said. My words came out quietly. "Why would she leave this house to me? Maybe it's a curse. She once said that the building caused her endless trouble. I

33

caused her a lot of difficulties, for sure. Maybe this is her way of getting back at me, and now I'll find out what it's like to be a landlord of a decayed building. Now the other tenants will shout at me instead of her. Maybe, in a way, it's a form of revenge."

"And maybe it's love." Claire spoke softly. The determined, assured tone was still there but it was no longer dominant. It was suffused with a gentleness which had always been there, but which she had never acknowledged. Now it was finally coming to the surface. She looked directly at me as she spoke.

"What do you mean?" I asked.

"She was lonely, you know."

"I know," I said. "You're the one who told me she didn't have any children. Who knows? Maybe she adopted me in a strange sort of way. I sure filled up her time with all our arguments. I gave her something to do, I suppose."

"She admired you too, you know."

"What do you mean?"

"She was proud of you, Ben. She was proud because you were a scholar, an educated person. She told me about all the books she had seen lining your shelves, that you were a professor. She said these things as if she was proud of you, as if she was talking about a son."

I was silent again, thinking. She both loved me and hated me. Every parent wants to leave their child something. I suppose this house was all she had, and now it was mine. It was a crummy, old house and I would end up having the same problems with it that she did. But it was also a bequest, a gift—all she had to give.

Finally, looking at Claire, I said, "You know, I'm sorry she's gone. She wasn't really a bad person. She's probably seen many hard times, harder than I'll ever experience. I'm sorry she didn't get to enjoy life more. It was her right. It's everybody's, isn't it?"

"Yes, it is, Ben," Claire answered. She spoke softly. Then she was silent. We sat again, without speaking, in the dark living room. I could not tell if she had truly meant what she said, or had just said it to agree with me, to make me feel better.

That night Claire stayed with me. It was the first time in two years. I suppose it was her way of acknowledging the great sadness that had come upon me. The silence was only broken at two in the morning by an upstairs neighbour calling to tell me that a pipe had broken and would I call a plumber immediately.

Alleywalk

WE WOULD USUALLY start out at one or two in the morning—
me and my friend Peter, that is. We would choose the longest alley
we could find. Some went for a mile or two before they were cut
off by a factory or large building. These Montreal alleys were, of
course, silent at night, and they weren't illuminated in any way. It
was just us, and the occasional alley cat. And of course, the garbage. A thousand miles of shattered bottles and rain-soaked
newspapers. The cats really were pitiful. Their fur was ragged and
dishevelled and they were terrified of us. Poor animals. We didn't
want to harm them.

But we enjoyed the solitude of the night. When we walked
through these dark alleys we could experience the quiet of the city
and know that we were alone and no one could touch us. At first
we would walk silently. But we were both story-tellers and soon it
would come out—the tales of adventure, about canoe trips in
northern Quebec and gondola rides in New Mexico and, inevitably, the talk about love and feelings and pain. The night, with all
its silence and all its clarity, brought it out of us. Sometimes our
lives seemed so complicated. Why did we do it to ourselves?

We would walk until three or four in the morning. Once we
walked till dawn, all the way to the docks. The alleys ended in the
centre of the city but it didn't matter because in the early morning
the downtown area was almost deserted. We sat by the river,
beside the grain elevators and warehouse buildings, quietly smok-
ing cigarettes, observing a silence that matched the mood of the
city. Eventually, though, we were disturbed by the large trucks
that began pulling up, bringing their noise and dust. We got up
and took the first run of the eighty bus back to our neighbour-

hood and said good-bye. We could rest at last.

I occasionally go to New York to visit my friend Floyd. He has been around the world twice and now works as a welder in a factory. He is also a poet and perhaps that is why, like me, he is cursed, or perhaps blessed by this restlessness which expresses itself with an urge to walk through the city at night. It is a special time, these early morning hours, a time when this mammoth city becomes our friend—a mysterious, formidable, even sinister friend—but our friend nevertheless. The empty streets, the all-night bars, the alleys and trash cans, the hookers quickly running in or out of taxicabs, the winos huddled in the corners, the alley rats—all form a peculiar fellowship of the night. And although we do not usually communicate with the other night people when we pass them in the street, we do glance at them, just as they glance at us. There is no danger. We understand each other.

We started out one night around one o'clock. It was mid-November and was fairly cold. We decided to walk up W. 112th Street. Floyd took a revolver out of his dresser drawer before we started but I said that I did not think it was necessary to take a weapon. I wasn't afraid. Floyd said, "O.K." and with a shrug replaced it in the drawer.

We walked briskly at first. There was a fair amount of traffic in the street but the sidewalks were bare. All the doors were bolted. We did not speak much while we walked but after about twenty minutes I heard Floyd shout, "Hey man, slow down." I realized that I was walking very quickly, too quickly for his comfort. I must have been caught up in my thoughts and not have noticed.

"I'm sorry," I said. I immediately slowed down and we walked at a more leisurely pace.

About an hour later we came upon a young lady, about twenty-five, sitting in a recessed doorway, playing with a cat. She was saying, "Here cat, here kitty," and the cat was slowly inching towards her, staring at her, perhaps as fascinated with her as I was. I watched the lady for a couple of minutes. She noticed me, but paid no attention. I was glad that she wasn't frightened of me and that I did not disturb her.

37

Three blocks further down we came upon some sort of theatre performance happening in a street level storefront. The
audience was facing out towards the street. The people were
nicely dressed. The men were wearing suits, some of the women
wore gowns. In front of them, before the window, facing the
audience, was the performance, I suppose. A boy was sitting in a
captain's chair wearing what looked like a toga. Chained to the
chair was a white goat, eating lettuce spread out all over the floor.
The audience was motionless, and expressionless. Floyd and I
stood in front of the window observing the audience and the goat.
Then it occurred to me that some people in the audience were
watching us. We were part of the spectacle. That made me feel
uncomfortable. It was like we were being ripped off. I said to
Floyd. "Come on, let's go," and we turned and continued walking.

As we walked we noticed a glow, about a block away. It
looked like a fire. We kept on walking, curious. As we approached
we looked into a courtyard where the light was coming from.
There, three black kids, two guys and a girl were standing around
a trash can that they had started a fire in. We stood on the side-
walk, looking in at the courtyard for a moment.

"Hey, man," one of the guys shouted, "you part of them
folks out there, y'know, with the goat?"

We were surprised. Neither of us expected the kid to talk to
us. The other guy and girl were silent. They looked at us blankly.
But we had been asked a question. I had always felt an obligation
to reply to any query, regardless of who it had come from.

"No, we don't have anything to do with them," I answered.

We stood silently again, for a moment. There is something
transfixing about a fire at night, doubly so when in the centre of
the city where it does not belong.

The young black kid who had spoken to us must have caught
my gaze at the fire. He beckoned:

"Hey, man. C'mon and get your hands warm. It's cold out
there."

I looked at Floyd. He was silent. Maybe he was thinking
about the gun he had left behind.

The black kid saw us hesitating. "C'mon man, you shy or
something?" he shouted.

I looked at Floyd again. He shrugged as if to say, "It's your show." But I knew he would follow if I went in. We stick together.

It was only about twenty feet to the kids. We entered the laneway to the courtyard and stopped at the fire. They were mostly burning garbage but there was also some wood in the can from packing crates they had broken up. We could feel the heat emanating from the walls of the metal trash can. It was a type of giant radiator.

We stood there with the kids. The girl was motionless. The two guys were holding their hands out towards the fire, shifting their weight, slightly but constantly. They looked to be around eighteen.

We stood together without speaking for couple of minutes. I put up my hands towards the fire and Floyd soon did the same. The silent girl and guy sometimes peeked at us, but most of the time during this quiet interlude they kept their gaze on the fire. But I caught their glances. They were probably more suspicious of us than we were of them. "Shit, man," I imagined the silent guy saying to himself. "What's he doing asking these white dudes in here? What's he trying to prove anyway?"

Then the bold kid broke the silence.

"Where you come from?" he asked, looking at me.

"Montreal," I answered.

"Oh yeah," he said. "It's cold up there, huh?"

"Yeah," I answered. "Pretty cold, all right."

"How 'bou you?" he said, raising his head towards Floyd.

"New York," answered Floyd laconically without looking away from the fire. He wasn't very talkative.

The bold kid shuffled his feet. Then he took a flask from the side pocket of his jacket and extended it to me.

"What's in it? I asked, trying to be cautious.

"Don't worry man," he said. "It's good. Drink some."

I took it from him, uncapped it, and had a drink. It tasted like gin. Could have been wood alcohol though, or anything. I gave it back to the kid and he extended it to Floyd. Floyd said, "No thanks." The kid didn't seem offended. He took it back and took a swig himself. Then he returned it to his pocket. I suppose his two companions didn't drink.

We stood again, in silence, by the fire, hands extended, shifting our weight slowly from foot to foot.

"What'd ya think? It's nice out this time of night, huh?" said the kid again.

"It sure is," I replied. "Nicest time in the city."

"Yeah," he said. "We like it. Nobody around to bother us."

"What do you do during the day?" I asked.

"Not much. Just hang loose. She's takin' it easy," he said gesturing towards the girl. "She's gonna have a baby."

At that moment she looked up at him, then turned silently away. I stared at her for a moment getting the feeling she resented the kid's remark.

"You go to school?" I asked.

"Fuck school," said the kid abruptly.

His other male companion snickered. It was his first real response to me. I felt I had asked a stupid question.

We stood for a while by the fire without speaking. Then the kid took out his flask again and handed it to me. I took another swig and handed it to Floyd who now also took a drink, a deep one, and smacked his lips. Then Floyd passed it to the silent kid who took a drink and handed it to the girl who also drank. It was a kind of midnight communion, a consummation of some sort.

The five of us became silent again, as we stared at the fire. I could feel the strong liquor working its way through me.

A minute later I looked at Floyd. I could tell it was now time for us to go. I said good-night to the talkative kid and glanced at the other two. All three said good-night in return, looking at us with a friendly form of acknowledgement. As we turned to leave the silent kid said softly. "You be careful now, huh." It was the first time he had spoken.

I turned to him and said. "I'll try man, I'll try."

We walked back, along the same route. The storefront was now empty. The girl with the cat had disappeared. I missed her. The only people we passed in the street were a couple of winos stumbling along.

We arrived at Floyd's one-room apartment around four in the morning. Floyd got into the bed. I lay out on the sofa.

"You know," I said to him before closing my eyes, "I suppose it's a curse we've got, huh? But it's not such a bad curse."

"No, it isn't," he replied. "I'm just glad I don't have to work tomorrow."

"Me too," I said. "Me too."

World of Women

ME AND MY FRIEND Peter bought a smoked whitefish at the kosher bakery, just before closing. It was Friday evening, in the middle of a very hot July. The fish was already cooked and looked pretty good to eat. Peter carried it close to him. It was wrapped in brown wax paper.

We started walking home through the alleys where we could be alone. We often felt most comfortable there. We were away from the city a little bit, the traffic and other people.

As we walked we passed a small ledge, beside a submerged coal cellar. I suggested we sit down. Nobody uses coal any more. The ledge wasn't too dirty. Peter agreed. He would have done almost anything I suggested. His will was gone.

"When I was a kid I played all the time in these alleys," I said. "Once I got together with another kid. We pooled our money and bought half a watermelon at the corner grocer. Took it down to the alley and sat on a ledge just like this. Didn't have a knife so we cracked it open by smashing it on the pavement and broke it apart with our hands."

Peter didn't answer. He just stared ahead.

"You want to eat the fish?" I asked.

Peter said O.K. and unwrapped it. We picked at it with our fingers. It tasted good, slightly sweet. It was Friday night.

"You should forget her," I said.

Peter sat silently. He was looking in at himself. Then he said, "You should get a double bed."

"What?"

"You should get a double bed. Before I got a double bed I lost so many girlfriends. You need room to move around."

"A single bed gives out a different message," I said.

"What message?"

"It's like I look more sincere, more ascetic, you know. She sees a single bed and says, 'hey, maybe he doesn't sleep around with everyone he meets. Maybe he's waited for someone like me.' "

"Get a double bed," he said again. "It'll be a lot less trouble."

"Maybe you're right."

We sat again without speaking. How do you console someone? We ate slowly, picking the flesh off the bones. It was very filling. Lots of good protein.

"If you don't forget her you'll just become sick," I finally said.

Peter continued looking ahead.

"And what about your poetry? How're you going to write that? By moping around and looking at your feet?"

"She inspired me. She typed out all my manuscripts."

"You'll find someone else. There's a world of women out there."

"I know there is."

I was glad he agreed. There was some hope, at least.

Dusk was falling now. It was darker in the alley and it began to feel a bit strange sitting on the ledge. The alley really now belonged to the wailing cats and other creatures of the night. The fish was finished now, too. All that was left was the skeleton.

"You can sleep at my house, if you want," I said. "It'll be less lonely. We can watch T.V."

"Thanks. Maybe I will."

Then Peter rose slowly. "Let's go," he said.

"You want to walk by the alley or the street?"

"By the street," he said, "Where there's a lot of people. We can listen to the music coming out of the clubs. There's a new lady singing at the Mirage."

"That's fine by me," I said. It was now my turn to agree. The street with its coloured neons, and noise and people sounded pretty good.

Bedclothes

AFTER I BOUGHT my double bed I continued to use the covers from my old single bed. I never really thought of changing them— they were adequate for me.

But things change when someone else shares this precious sanctuary. Someone who likes to be well-covered, always warm. Toasty is the word, I suppose. Someone who doesn't like drafts or to have one bare leg exposed.

I realized a problem was at hand—but I didn't realize the gravity until she began to cry out (is shriek the word?) "You're taking all the blankets." And I had no defence because in reality, in my unconscious sleep I was taking all the blankets. I'm a sort of tall guy who moves around in his sleep and the blankets were not that big and they just seemed to wrap themselves around me, swaddle me, in the course of the night, leaving her exposed to the night-time air.

And then one night after a couple of moans, and somnolent shrieks about blankets she said in her half-sleep, "I'm going to sleep on the sofa from now on." And panic struck. She would sleep on the sofa—I would lose my lover. Terror.

The next day was a time for action. I got in my car and went down to Grand Draperies on the main street where two of my Polish volleyball teammates worked as salesmen. I had never bought blankets before—this was a new adventure. There were discreet inquiries about double or queen size blankets. The old owner of the store approached and asked, "What do you need really big blankets for if you're not married?" All I could do was smile coyly. To him it was a reasonable question.

I settled on two summer blankets, two wool winter blankets and a flannel sheet. I thought of getting a big comforter but it was so slippery that I was sure it would slide off the bed and that was definitely what I did not need.

The next time I saw her she acknowledged the new purchase graciously. But our problems were not really over. I still had a tendency to pull the blankets over to one side. And when I crawled into bed I would raise the blankets and create a draft which would generate another shriek. The double flannel sheet shrunk away to the size of a handkerchief on the first washing. But we gradually adjusted. I created fewer drafts, pulled the blankets less over to my side, and didn't even mind the night when she left the bed to sleep in the sleeping bag on the living room floor.

And I suppose that is the point of the story. Because the next morning I awoke at seven (I had to leave the house at eight), and saw her lying under the sleeping bag, in my torn blue pyjamas, catching the morning light from the window, looking so warm and soft and rosy-cheeked and relaxed in the old sleeping bag. And she called to me before I left and I regret I did not have time to crawl into that sanctuary with her and feel her warmth beside me.

Two Year's Absence

IT WAS FOUR in the morning when Bill finally arrived at his parents' home. It wasn't a very good time to arrive. But the weather had been bad, fog and autumn rain, and then the fan belt on his truck had broken and he had been forced to stop by the side of the road to fix it. On entering the city he had also taken a wrong turn on the expressways that ringed it. It was two years since he had been home and he had lost his familiarity with its enveloping highways. But he eventually sorted his directions out and found his parents' house in their silent night-time neighbourhood.

On driving through it he could not help but remark how plain and uncommitted this neighbourhood still appeared to be. It wasn't a slum, it certainly wasn't for those with even a modicum of wealth. The two-storey row house flats that lined its streets lacked balconies or any ornamentation to break their plain, brick facades. They were the homes of the middle people, the in-between people, those who were grateful to live in an area of the city that was at least clean and where they could have a small lawn with a tree and perhaps a garden in back. Many, too, were homes of old people, the fearful ones, those who were certain to lock their doors at all times and who peeked out from behind lace curtains with curiosity and apprehension at any new activity in the street.

He parked the black pickup truck and removed the house key from his pocket. He had held onto it for these two years knowing he would eventually return. He slung his small A-frame knapsack over one shoulder, walked up to the house and opened the front door. All the lights were out, of course. His plan had been to quietly go to sleep on the sofa and then see his parents in the morning, but being thirsty from the journey he left his knapsack by the door and walked into the kitchen where he turned on a light.

The kitchen was spotless. The arborite counters gleamed just as they had two years before. No scrap of food, no stray cup or dish lay about. He felt his mother's presence in that kitchen. She had devoted her life to the small world of order. The two were inseparable. On opening the refrigerator he noticed that, as in the past, it was still stocked with food. Bill wondered why there had always been so many provisions in the refrigerator for two old people. It must have gone back to his mother's remembrance of the hard times she had experienced during the war in Europe. A full refrigerator was a statement for her he supposed, a solace, or reminder. He removed a bottle of ginger ale, poured himself a glass and began sipping it as he leaned back against a kitchen counter.

As he drank, his father, grey-haired, in his pyjamas, appeared in the doorway. He was smiling, happy and surprised at seeing his son.

"Hi, hi," said his father.

Bill remembered his father's particular greeting. He had always said "hi" twice, the second time replacing the embrace or simple handshake that would have been appropriate instead.

"Hi, dad," answered Bill. It felt good to see his father. He looked well. Bill walked up to him and warmly grasped his father's right hand between his own two hands.

"So," said his father. How's our traveller?"

"He's fine, Dad. I'm sorry I'm so late. I was delayed on the road. Nothing to worry about. Did you get my letter?"

"Yes. Of course. Your mother must have read it four or five times."

"How is she?"

"She's fine. But she's sleeping. Move quietly, O.K."

"All right. I'll be careful."

They were both quiet for a moment, examining each other as two people often do after a long absence.

"So, you must have a lot of stories to tell," said his father.

"Yes," said Bill. "I do."

His father hesitated. Then he said, "Well not tonight. Tomorrow's a better time, you know."

"I understand," said Bill. "I'll tell you about a lot of things later. I've seen some beautiful places."

Then they were silent again. It was as in the past. Neither was sure what to say to the other.

Soon his father moved over to the refrigerator and removed some chocolate cake resting on a plate.

"Here," he said, laying it on the counter. "Your mother made this yesterday. It's good. Have some."

"All right." Bill removed a knife and fork from a drawer and a plate from a cupboard and cut himself a slice.

You want some?" he asked, while placing the cake on his plate.

"Oh, no. It's too late for me. But go ahead. It's good."

Bill took his ginger ale and cake, sat down at the kitchen table, and began eating slowly. His father stood silently, watching him.

"It's good," said Bill.

"Yes, Mom makes good cakes," said his father.

He continued to watch him while he ate. Bill liked feeling his father's presence. He wished they had more to say.

Finally he looked up and said, "You look tired, Dad. You should go to bed. I'll sleep on the sofa."

"I'll get you some blankets."

"No," said Bill. "Don't bother. I have a sleeping bag. I'll be fine."

Are you sure?"

"Yes. Of course. Don't worry."

"O.K." said his father. "Have a good night." Then almost as an afterword he added, "Move quietly, all right, not to wake your mother."

Don't worry, I'll move carefully."

His father left the room. Bill sat quietly. Words aren't all that necessary, he thought. I felt his presence. That's more important, isn't it? But in reality he wasn't at all sure if that was more important. He just wasn't sure. He finished the cake, put the dish and fork in the sink and replaced the rest of the cake in the refrigerator. Then he turned out the light, making sure that he walked softly, so as not to disturb anyone.

The next four days were times to sit about the kitchen table with his parents and tell stories about travels in a truck, about New Mexico and South Dakota and small lonely towns in the Midwest, and about communes and the people he had spent time with along the way. His father listened carefully. Bill knew his father could not understand the attraction he felt to these travels, the necessity he felt for them, but in his old world politeness and pleasure at being with his son he listened dutifully to his stories. His mother, on the other hand, would interrupt. She expressed shock that he often slept on the ground and warned him about arthritis. And she asked him about girls. Had he met any nice ones along the way? Bill would nod and say he had, and not comment any further.

They were times too for Bill to observe his parents, to come to know them once again. They were a bit greyer, perhaps their faces were more lined. His father was seventy, his mother sixty-five. But they were aging well and he was glad to see that they were still in good health, still working—his mother around the house, his father in his small fruit store down the block.

In the afternoons he began helping his father in the store. He unpacked crates, arranged produce, sold to customers. Some of the customers who came into the store remembered him from the time when he was a high school student and had helped his father after school and during vacations. They inquired curiously of him, in their old people's way, where he had been. Was he going to stay in town and look for a job? Was he married?

The store, like his parents, had barely changed. His father still calculated bills on an old adding machine and made change from a wooden drawer underneath the counter. The tiny shop, not much larger than a living room, was an anachronism in this day. There was a large supermarket four blocks away. But the older people in the neighbourhood had remained faithful to the store and would often drop in to buy something, if only a quart of milk, or half dozen eggs. If they were short of cash, if a pension cheque had not arrived, they could buy what they wished and his father would write their name on the back of a cash slip to save in the wooden drawer and they would repay him the next time they came in. Some of the younger people from the neighbourhood also used the store and would often scurry through on their way home from work to buy a newspaper or a few small items. Bill liked the store, its aroma, the people who passed through to chat. He wore an old, stained white apron while he worked, probably the same one he had worn years before. It was a type of uniform and he still took a certain pride in it. In mid-afternoon he would take a five minute break and sit on an old, upright coke crate and drink cold apple juice.

On the third morning of his return he sat, as in previous mornings, in the kitchen reading the morning paper while his mother washed the breakfast dishes. His father was already in the store but his parents had insisted that he sleep in and take his time in the mornings. Relieving him of obligations was their way of honouring him as a guest, and it was for the same reason that his mother refused to let him help her prepare breakfast or wash the dishes. It was while she worked at the sink that Bill heard her say:

"I don't know. I'm an old lady. I don't know things anymore."

"What do you mean?" he asked, looking up.

"You know what I mean. In my time a young man grew up, finished school if he could, got a job, married. Everybody wanted to settle down. It was what you were supposed to do."

"I know," said Bill. "A lot of people do things differently these days."

"Sure, now people get divorced, have affairs, stay single because they're in love with a career instead. But deep down they all want the same things, don't they? A home and family."

"Most people probably do."

"And there's nothing wrong with it, is there?"

"Of course not."

"You know, a lot of your friends from school got married. Your father and I, sometimes we see them in the park on Sundays when they have concerts. Some of them look so nice, with good clothes and their wives holding their arms. Some have children and they bring them along. They've done well, you know. They have professions. One's a doctor."

50

"That's great," said Bill. He didn't say it with sarcasm.

"And what about you?" said his mother.

"What do you mean?"

"You know what I mean. Your father and me, we're old now. Thank God your father can still work in the store and we get pensions too. But you," she said, looking directly at him, "you're the young one. Now's the time to think about building something."

"Come on," said Bill. "You should realize already that I'm not about to live my life just to please you. I'm doing what I want. And if planting trees three months a year in British Columbia is what I want then that's what I'll do. Take a good look. I'm healthy, pretty strong. I know how to build a log house, harvest wheat, even take care of a whole herd of goats. I didn't know these things before and now I do. I never take money that isn't earned. I support myself. I even pay taxes. It's not a bad life and..." Bill stopped in mid-sentence. He realized he was preaching and felt awkward. He had no need to justify himself to anyone. After a moment he said, "I'm sorry, Mom. I haven't seen you for two years. Let's not argue. Not now."

"I didn't mean to cause any arguments," said his mother. "I just want the best for you."

"I know," he said. "Don't worry. Everything will be fine." Then he rose from the table, kissed his mother and said, "I'm going off to work now. I think I'll go to a movie tonight so don't worry about supper." Then he left the house.

He felt badly as he walked along, sorry he had raised his voice, sorry his mother had forced him to. He had truly wanted to see his family again. And he had wanted it to be simple, without consequences.

As he walked along he began to think back to the time when he was sixteen and had first left his family. He had walked out of this same house in their north Toronto neighbourhood, taken a city bus to the highway and hitchhiked to Winnipeg. While there he slept in a hostel, one of many that the government had set up for young people who were travelling across the country. When he arrived he called his parents. They were distraught. His mother was crying. Bill told them about a book on Zen he had read which discussed children and referred to them as visitors in a home, to be treated as honoured guests. And just as one was not meant to cling to a guest, so was one not meant to attach oneself to a child. It all seemed so simple. He hoped they would understand.

He returned home ten days later, hitchhiking, stopping off in small towns along the way. Once he worked as a dishwasher in a small restaurant on the road. The cook was a large Greek man who told Bill stories about Greece and the beautiful sun that shone down on the Aegean islands. Bill enjoyed listening to his stories while he worked with him in the kitchen and felt sorry that the cook had exiled himself to such a distant, cold country.

When he returned home his parents greeted him warmly, inquired about his health, told him they had worried about him. But they did not greet him with the same passion, and possession that had been so much a part of their relationship before. Bill actually missed their fondling but realized he could not return to the past. His childhood had irrevocably ended.

After finishing university he took a job selling industrial equipment. He earned a good living, had a car, a nice apartment, a number of casual affairs. One June day, on his twenty-seventh birthday he left his suburban work place at five o'clock as usual, and stepped into the warm sun. He was wearing a jacket and tie. Summer was just beginning. He walked through the parking lot, to his car and when he reached it removed his keys from his pocket. It was the brightest day that month and the sun's light was reflected with almost blinding intensity off the asphalt. He hesitated before opening the car door and instead remained standing erect on this black pavement divided by its regular yellow lines. He was clutching the keys tightly in his palm, squinting in the sun which continued to beat down on this flat suburban industrial park landscape. A few people leaving the factory walked by. Some nodded to him but he perceived them only as indistinct, shimmering figures, each one anonymous. When he finally opened his fist it was fifteen minutes later. He noticed that he had clutched the keys so tightly that they had left deep indentations in his hand. "It doesn't matter," he said to himself. "They'll go away. Everything goes away." He then stepped into the car and turned on the ignition. The engine sounded smooth, gentle. He realized that he had never looked forward as much to moving in a car. When he reached the exit of the parking lot he turned right instead of left, the direction he usually took which led back to the city. Once on the highway he opened all the windows of the car to let the air rush through. He was now moving in a direction that was already far from home. In Minnesota he traded in the car at a roadside lot for the black pick-up truck. He thought that, somehow, it might be more useful on his journey. And he kept on driving, down through the farms and ranchlands of the Midwest, the forests of the Pacific northwest and the gold mines of Alaska and the Yukon, through the vast North American landscape that seemed now to be his only home. He would stop along the way, spend time with some fine people, and others who were not so good, share their food and labour, but always pass through, never settle too long in any one place.

In northern Ontario, two years later, he spent Thanksgiving with a family he had met along the way. Steven was a homesteader who had left the city with his wife Giselle and two small children, Ivan and Metrayea. Giselle later explained to Bill that Metrayea, the name of their daughter and younger child meant the coming Buddha. They lived on an eight acre farm where they raised sheep and occasionally worked in nearby sawmills to raise extra money. Bill spent two weeks with them, helping to cut wood for the upcoming winter, and to build the extra room they were adding to their house. Steven was a rugged person and Bill liked working with him outside in the cold air. On Thanksgiving the family had a large traditional dinner. After eating they sat around the kitchen table and read short stories and poems aloud to each other. The wood stove warmed the house with a comforting, radiant heat and the words reverberated gently, distinctly in the northern night. They became a sort of lullabye for the children who soon dozed off.

After Steven and Giselle had put the children to bed and gone to sleep themselves Bill stayed up and stoked the stove, to make sure the fire would last through the night. Then, after spreading out his own sleeping bag on the plywood platform that served as his bed, he began to think of his own family whom he had not seen in two years. He was no more than four hundred miles from them. It was possible that he could visit them.

Three days later when he told his hosts that he would be leaving they both said that he wasn't imposing on them at all and that he was welcome to stay with them through the winter if he wished. The children liked him and he could help with the farm and in finishing off the new room. Bill thanked them. Perhaps on his way back from the city he would stop off.

Before leaving, Steven gave him a gift of a bone handled sheath knife. The blade was made from carbon steel, the best there was. But he warned him that it had to be cared for carefully. Bill thanked him and assured him he would keep it dry and oiled. He then exchanged kisses and handshakes and gave both children warm hugs. As he drove away from their house, along the dirt road on their land he glanced in the rear view mirror and saw Metrayea waving at him. She continued waving until he turned the bend on to the spruce forest road that would eventually take him to the highway.

On the third day of this return to his family Bill came home from the store at six-thirty as usual. He had spent much of the afternoon building wooden display bins for his father so that he would not have to leave so much of the produce in wooden packing crates on the floor. His father had at first said that the old way was good enough but Bill had convinced him that the new bins would save space and be more efficient. He arrived home tired, his clothes covered in sawdust, carrying his apron for his mother to wash.

On entering the house he heard the voices of two women coming from the kitchen. He stepped inside, still carrying the stained apron rolled into a small bundle. His mother was sitting at the kitchen table with a slim young lady. The apparent guest, who seemed to be about twenty-five, was dressed in a fashionable skirt, nylon stockings, pointed high heeled shoes. She was wearing eye shadow and mascara. Bill noticed especially that her fingernails were long and painted a deep red. He had always disliked make-up, considering it artificial and unnecessary.

"There you are, Bill," his mother said as he entered the kitchen. "I want you to meet Violet. We've just been talking all about the hospital where she works. She's a nurse. I've asked her to stay for supper. I hope you don't mind."

Bill stood silent for a moment, examining Violet, his mother, the special plates on the table each with a cloth napkin and polished silverware alongside.

"No, I don't mind," he said in a low voice that did not disguise his suspicion. Then, extending his apron to his mother he said, "Here, this has to be washed."

"Leave it in the hamper, and I'll do it tomorrow. Where's your father?"

"He's in the store finishing the cash. He'll be here in a few minutes."

After another brief pause he said, "Well...I better go change."

"Fine," said his mother. "We'll eat as soon as your father gets home."

Violet was the first to speak to Bill when they were all gathered around the table. It was just after his mother had served the first course.

"I understand you travel a lot," she said.

"Yes," answered Bill laconically, without expression.

"You must enjoy it," she said.

"It's all right," answered Bill with the same flat tone.

Violet became silent. Neither of his parents spoke. Bill felt uncomfortable. Perhaps he had been unkind in his abruptness. There was no point hurting her, he thought.

"Do you like travelling?" he asked. The question was prosaic but it seemed to suit the awkwardness of the general setting.

"I love travelling on my vacations," she said. "Last winter I went to Hawaii. And in a couple of months I'm going to Las Vagas. Frank Sinatra's singing there. I adore him."

"My God," thought Bill. "What's going on here?"

"Do you like music?" continued Violet.

"Oh, yeah," answered Bill. He suddenly spoke in a more animated voice. "A while ago I heard this really great punk group in Chicago called The Stamps. They do this neat number on stage where they kill a frog."

Silence descended on the table. Violet looked down at her place setting. Bill felt bad that he had had to express his displeasure at the whole affair in such a crude manner. After a few moments, however, his mother broke the embarrassed silence. She began serving a new course and while doing that struck up a conversation with Violet, and was soon joined by his father. They talked about hospitals, doctors, medical problems, gossipped about the neighbourhood. They were genuinely enjoying each other's company. Bill was glad. It was good for his parents to have another young person in the house. He still remained detached, though, relieved that the success of the evening no longer depended on him.

After dessert and tea Violet said that she would have to leave as she worked early the next day. Bill's father volunteered to help her on with her coat in the vestibule. In her momentary absence Bill's mother asked him in the kitchen, in a low voice so as not to be overheard, to walk her home.

"Why?" he asked. "She lives nearby."

"Never mind why," said his mother. "It won't hurt you. Be a gentleman."

When Violet returned with her coat Bill volunteered to accompany her.

"It's not necessary," she said in a low voice while buttoning the coat. She avoided looking at him.

"No, I'd like to," he said.

"All right," said Violet perfunctorily, still without looking at him.

It was about two-and-a-half blocks to Violet's apartment building. Neither spoke as they walked along the first block. As they approached the second Bill's eye was caught by a Jeep parked nearby. It was a rather fancy model with a large eagle painted on the hood. Violet also glanced at it and said, "Nice car, isn't it, the Renegade?"

Bill noticed that she referred to the vehicle by its model name, as if it were a showpiece. To him it was nothing more than a Jeep, good for getting out of snow and mud. There were many times in his travels that he had wished he had a vehicle like that.

Neither spoke as they walked along the second block. Bill did not look at Violet at all.

As they approached the third block, Violet broke the silence.

"I know you don't like me," she said. "I didn't want to make you uncomfortable. Your mother invited me. I like her. I did it more for her."

Bill stopped and turned to her. They were now in front of her apartment building. For the first time that evening he truly felt like speaking.

"It's not your fault," he said. "I acted rudely. I'm sorry."

"Don't worry about it," she said. "You weren't expecting me. It must have been an imposition on you. Anyway, can I wish you well on your travels?"

"Of course, I'd like to wish you well too. Hope you like Vegas."

"I'm sure I will. Maybe you should go sometime. You might like it."

"I've passed through a couple of times. Hated it."

"Well. . . I love it," she said with a confident smile. Then she said good-bye and walked up to the entrance of her apartment building. Before she opened the door Bill called to her:

"Violet, you know that band in Chicago, with the frog?"

"Yes," she said, turning around.

"They were terrible," he said.

Violet smiled again and waved to him. Bill waved back. Then she went inside.

As he walked back home along the silent evening streets he could not help thinking about the brief time he had spent in Kentucky, in the hill country among poor people—miners and small farmers. He had stayed with a lady he had met, Anita. She was twenty-seven and wasn't especially pretty, at least in the fashionable sense. She was thin and rather flat-chested and had a slightly hollowed in face covered with freckles. She certainly never wore any make-up. She had been raised in that district but had left for a while, had gone to college where she became a nurse, spent time in larger cities up north. Now she had come back to work as a midwife. She was quite sophisticated, in the urban sense, but still felt very much at home in this land among its poor people, their conservative ways. Bill remembered the ankle-length frilled dresses that she wore. He used to call them her hippy dresses. They were her strongest affectation. He still remembered sitting in the cabin watching from a window as she returned home from work carrying her bag of instruments, walking along the muddy road that led up to their home.

Sometimes Bill would accompany her on her midwife calls. Most of the patients were black. They were poor and often lived in decayed shacks. Twice he stayed through the night while she delivered a baby. He remained in a separate room, with the men and children where the grown-ups shared stories, passed a bottle of whisky. They were always silent when the birthing woman screamed in her labour, and then quickly began talking again, about anything, as if to reassure themselves that everything was all right and to shut out the pain of the one so close by.

In the third week of this stay with her he told Anita that he loved her. It was a long time since he had said that to a woman and he truly meant it. Anita replied that it felt good to hear. Bill continued that he loved her enough to marry her. Anita said she was flattered. But they both had to be realistic. She knew he would not want to settle down in this poor hill country. And she would not want to leave. She had come back for a purpose. Bill said that he worried about her living alone in the cabin with only a wood stove, no hot water or even a proper toilet. But she reassured him that she had been fine till then and would be fine in the future. He knew she would. Before he left he promised to return. She was the only person he had ever asked to marry.

When Bill returned from walking Violet home he found his parents seated in the living room watching television. His mother called to him as he entered.

"So," she said.

"So, what?" asked Bill.

"So, what do you think? She's a nice girl, isn't she?"

"Yes, she is," he answered.

"Do you think you'll see her again?"

"I don't know. Probably not."

"Why not? I think she's pretty. And she dresses so nicely."
Yeah, she is pretty."

"And . . ."

Bill walked up to her and squatted down beside the large armchair she was seated in.

"I want to thank you, Mom, for introducing her to me. But I didn't come back to meet anyone new."

"What's wrong with getting acquainted with another person? It won't hurt you. I like Violet. She's very nice and polite and has a job."

"And she's in love with Frank Sinatra and Las Vagas and fancy cars."

"So, what are you? A snob? Lots of people like Frank Sinatra. Besides, he's a very good singer."

"I'm different, that's all."

"All I wanted was for you to meet her, Bill. I see Violet in the stores around here and sometimes we talk a bit. She seemed so pleasant. I asked her to come over one evening and she said she would."

"I understand, Mom. But you shouldn't put people in awkward situations. You could end up hurting them. She could have been embarrassed."

"Don't push him," intruded Bill's father. "He's young. He has lots of time."

"Who's pushing? I just want him to be happy."

"When he wants to settle down, then he'll settle down. He'll come home and get a job and an apartment. And then he'll meet someone and you'll see, everything will be fine."

"You, you always have a solution. That's why you're so rich? That's why you run a fruit store instead of a supermarket."

"Come on," interrupted Bill loudly. "Don't start fighting now. I've only been home a week and everybody's going at each other."

His parents were still.

"This is all useless," he said. "It isn't what I came home for."

The next two days were quiet in the house. Bill worked in the store, went for walks in the evenings, out to a film once. He spoke to his parents only about ordinary matters dealing with the store or mundane household affairs.

On the third day he woke at five, as he often did when he lived in the country or travelled. It was a special time of day for him, a cross-over time when devotees in ashrams and monasteries were rising for their morning meditation, and others, often writers, artists, musicians, were finally going to bed after a night's work. He packed his few belongings carefully in the canvas A-frame knapsack and put it by the door. Then he went into the kitchen where he made a cup of tea and sat alone watching the dawn light slowly penetrate the room.

His father entered the kitchen at seven. It was part of his routine to rise around that time.

"You're up pretty early," he remarked.

"Yes. I'm leaving this morning. I wanted to get an early start."

"Leaving? But you've been here less than two weeks."

"I know. But I think it's best that I go. I'll be back. Don't worry."

"Do you know where you're going?"

"I thought I'd head out to Alberta. There's a man out there I can work for."

"But it's almost winter. It's freezing there."

"I can take it," said Bill, flexing his muscle in a mock gesture. "And in the spring I'm going to go to Kentucky. It'll be warm there. There's someone I want to see."

"I see...I see," said his father as he mulled over his son's departure. Then he said, "Do you need some money for your trip?"

"No, no, I'm fine."

Another hesitation followed after which his father said, "Thank you for helping in the store. The new bins work. I should have thought of them a long time ago."

"I'm glad they're useful."

"You're going to wait for Mom to wake up, aren't you?"

"I've written her a note. I don't want to make any scenes.

Maybe I'll telephone her from the road."

"Are you sure?"

"Yeah. I think it's best. Anyway, I better go now. I love you and Mom, you know. I'm sorry we ended up fighting."

"Aw, don't worry," he said. "Such things happen."

"Yeah," said Bill, feeling somewhat relieved by his father's comment. "I'll write you," he continued. "And if I get a chance I'll send you photographs."

"That would be nice. But don't forget to call. Your mother will worry."

"Then I will for sure."

He then grasped his father's hand and said, "I'll see you. Take special care of yourself." Then he walked to the front door, picked up his knapsack and left.

The street was still quiet when he stepped into the cab of his truck. The morning light had not completely obliterated the dull grey of dawn. It was a good time to leave. He looked forward to being on the highway. He knew that the road had a way of swallowing up disappointment, even sadness. For the past two years it had been his best friend. He knew, all too clearly, that it still was.

Women Who Live in Small Rooms

I LIKE WOMEN who live in small rooms. Sparse rooms, with no more space, no more possessions than are really necessary. I've always felt that there is something transcendent about one who can live with solitude and without material clutter. Spiritual is the word used most often today. At least, that's the way I've always felt about it.

Ann could have lived in a high rise apartment that spanned the views of the city. Or in a suburban bungalow surrounded by lawns and well kept people. She was smart enough. She was pretty enough; many men certainly wanted to spirit her away to their own entrapments. But she lived in one room on Clark Street. An anonymous street that nobody walked down unless they had to. Most of the other people in her building were old, tucked away on welfare, forgotten by friends, surviving on television and black tea.

In Ann's room everything fit. There were so few possessions; but they all had their place. It was a low room. Everything was kept close to the floor. There was only one chair, a straight-backed one made of hardwood. She kept it by the window. Sometimes, during the evening, she would sit in it and look out. There was a mattress on the floor, neatly made. Bookshelves that went up no more than two feet supported by red bricks she had gathered from a demolished apartment building down the block. And there was the record player. Not the "system" that we have adopted today. Rather, it was the kind of forty dollar phonograph that many of us had as children. It, too, sat on the floor, beside the neat stack of record albums. There was no rug. The room would have appeared so much larger, brighter, had the floor been sanded and varnished. But the hardwood slats had turned a dull greyish brown with age and Ann had left them that way. There was no phone either. If you wanted to see her, you had to come in person.

We wouldn't spend much time in her room. We would mostly go out to bars, restaurants, the theatre once or twice. Or to my house, which had all the possessions, all the comforts our age called for.

It would be foolish for me to say I loved her. Anyone who has created such a spare, some would call it barren, world for themselves would by nature keep even love to themselves. But hers was not an unkind distance. She was honest, in the quiet way she had. I did not wish to pry, and as long as that desire was absent there were few barriers.

Love, and the act of loving though, are very distinct. In that sparse room there was still the soft touch of another's hand, the comfort of one close to you through the long night, the cup of tea sweetened with honey in the morning. But there was no attachment. She needed, demanded, so little.

One evening, rather than going out, we stayed in her room. I sat on the mattress, my back against the wall. Ann sat in the chair by the window. She sat erect, with her hands neatly folded in her lap. Her head was turned slightly towards the window. She was still wearing the neat skirt she had worn at work, at her secretary's job, during the day. Her hair was tied up. Her profile was classic. Like one of the Greek statues we find in museums. Her nylon-stockinged legs were angled gracefully on the side of the chair.

She sat silently, as she often did after returning from a day's work. She did not mind the world of commerce and I knew she did her job responsibly. But at the end of the day she divested herself completely of its concerns. Sitting as she was was like a meditation. To remove the day and accept the soul of the room.

After awhile, she sat down beside me on the mattress. I put my arm around her and she nestled close. It felt good to hold her. But we were disturbed, or perhaps I should say, I was disturbed, by a knock at the door.

Ann rose slowly and answered it. An old lady, in a housecoat and slippers stood there. She was wheezing and coughing. A crumpled handkerchief was tightly held in her hand.

63

"I'm sorry," said the old lady.

"It's all right," answered Ann.

She took the lady by the arm and walked her slowly down the dimly lit corridor of the building to her apartment. Once inside Ann gently helped the lady into an armchair and then covered her legs with a blanket. Then she went into the kitchen, washed out a pot and boiled some milk. When it was ready she poured it into a cup and brought it to the lady, carefully putting it in her hands. The old lady drank it, cradling the cup in both trembling palms. Ann stayed with her as she drank, watching the cup to make sure it wouldn't slip. When the lady was finished Ann took the cup from her. Then, standing behind the chair, she began massaging the old lady's shoulders. The lady closed her eyes. She smiled.

"Bless you," she said, still with her eyes closed. "You're the best friend I ever had."

Soon she was asleep. Ann stopped massaging her, washed out the cup and pot and quietly left the room, carefully closing the door so as not to make any noise and wake her.

Back in her room she again lay near me on the mattress.

"Poor lady," she said. "Her family abandoned her. I'm really all she has." She sighed. I held her more tightly.

I often walk alone at night through the streets of the centre of the city. At times I walk along the residential streets, by now asleep and darkened. I cannot help but notice that on each street, no matter how late it is there is a light on in at least one window. Someone is awake, perhaps also in a small room, dreaming aloud, praying, maybe loving or crying with the tears of the night.

At other times, when I wish to feel the presence of people and traffic, I walk along main streets in the poor underbelly of the city. These are avenues lined with all-night cafeterias and gaudy neon signs and scattered with men and women lingering in doorways, seeking out their living from the commerce of the night. And above these signs and slow-moving traffic there are the old apartment buildings, mostly darkened, many abandoned. But there too one can see the occasional lighted room punctuating these monolithic structures. Sometimes you can catch a glimpse of a person walking by a window, perhaps some wisps of cigarette smoke, or the stacatto light from a television. And perhaps too, if you look carefully, and with belief, you can see a person draping another with a blanket, offering them a cup of tea, or touching them lightly on their shoulder as they offer them the slight comfort that they, and a small room, can provide.

A Small Crime

WHEN HE WAS NINE years old he was brought to the door by a policeman who kept one hand on his arm as if to stop him from running away. He had been caught writing with a crayon on a wall of the subway station and his parents were expected to discipline him. The entire rest of the day he stayed in his room waiting for his father to come home from the shirt factory. A slap in the face, he thought, perhaps that's all I'll get. And maybe no allowance for the coming week. Still, he could not help but be apprehensive.

At five thirty he heard the front door open. His mother was talking to his father. They talked for a long time, much longer than he felt was necessary. Then the family ate supper. He was not invited and he felt that his punishment had already started. This saddened him greatly because he enjoyed eating supper with his father and telling him about the day's adventure. He tried to pass the time by reading through his comic books, but he was anxious and could not follow one through from beginning to end. At seven o'clock he heard the television come on as the family sat down in the living room. Every so often someone changed a channel. By eight thirty night had fallen and he felt more alone than he had ever been at any time in his life. He looked out into the garden behind his room. He could see the outline of the young tree his grandfather had planted a month before. It was beginning to sprout leaves and he tried to decide how many it would have that summer. He decided on fifteen. That knowledge made him feel better. By nine o'clock he was feeling drowsy and had lain out on his bed.

Shortly afterwards his father came into the room and sat down on the bed. The boy sat up putting his feet over the side. His father looked at him then turned away clasping his hands together. The boy looked down at the floor the whole time.

"I remember when I left Romania," his father said. "I went to the train station in my town and had to sit in a special section for people who were emigrating from the country. There were many other people sitting there, and I remember how funny it was that we all looked the same with our best clothes and old suitcases almost bursting. But what I remember most of all were the walls. It seemed that every person who had ever sat in that part of the railway station had written on the wall his name, his home town and the new place to which he was going. I spent a long time reading all the names on the wall. Many towns were represented and I even recognized the names of some people with whom I had once been friends. And do you know what I did? I took out my pen, found a clear space on the wall and wrote my own name, my home town, and the date. But you see I did not write on the wall out of mischief. It was my own way of saying *this is who I am—now I am ending an old life and starting a new one.* Perhaps one day you will have the same reason. But as long as times are good and we are welcome here there are other and better ways of letting the world know who you are."

He put his hand on the boy's shoulder as if to say, "don't worry, everything is all right." Then he rose slowly and said: "Be good to your mother and me and leave the walls alone." Then he left the room.

The boy lay back on his bed. Ordinarily it took him only two or three minutes to fall asleep. That night he lay awake for almost half an hour.

Your Eighteenth Birthday Was a Long Time Ago

TWO YEARS AFTER Tony Pasquale arrived in Montreal from his native Calabria in southern Italy he opened a small restaurant on Fairmount Ave. near Clark, in the immigrant section of Montreal. The restaurant had been a Jewish snack bar before and Tony left all the fixtures and furnishings as they were. People sat on steel folding chairs and ate their carefully prepared linguine and stracciatella soup on the same uncovered, shaky bridge tables.

When Hyman Ellman was nineteen and a student of literature at McGill University he had a falling out with his parents, and rather than stay on in their home, took a room in a rooming house on Clark St. near Laurier. Bursaries and loans from the provincial government covered his expenses. Occasionally, tiring of the food in the school cafeterias or the Kraft dinners he prepared on the hotplate in his room, he would walk over to Tony's and eat supper there. Tony could see by the books he carried that he was a student and, as his restaurant had not yet established a clientele, was grateful for Hyman's patronage and always gave him a discount on meals. For Hyman it was two-fifty for all he could eat. He called Hyman "Le Professeur" and in his broken English and French Tony liked to talk politics and religion with him.

When Hyman was twenty-one and had graduated from university he took stock of where he stood. He was afraid that a degree in literature might not go far towards helping him earn a living and decided that it would be best to obtain aonther, more practical degree. His marks were good and he won a scholarship to do an M.B.A. at McGill. By then he had achieved a reconciliation with is parents. But he had grown accustomed to being alone and continued to live in his small room with his books. For diversion there was a twelve-inch black-and-white television and occasional dinners and conversations at Tony's.

When Elaine Fraser was eighteen and began studying art history at Concordia University she discovered that there was a whole new world in inner city Montreal, a world considerably more exciting and slightly more forbidding than the one she had grown up with in the far suburbs. And, shortly after meeting Hyman she began to include him in this new world.
She was cautious at first. But there was an attraction. It was probably because he demanded little from her that she felt safe with him. Most of the young men who approached her at the university seemed to have one main objective in mind—to sleep with her. Hyman, on the other hand, appeared content just with her company. There were walks on Fletcher's Field, inexpensive movies at the university film society, evenings of studying together in the library. Attractions do grow, though, even if they are muted, and after six months she began spending the occasional night with him in his tiny, crowded room. Her parents were not expecially pleased when, six months later, they decided to marry. She was barely nineteen. But he did seem bright. He was close to finishing his second degree and was becoming something of an expert in business systems. Unlike other students they had heard about in the media of the 1960s, he wasn't a bum. He had a future. They extracted only one promise from him, aside from the one that he take good care of her. They made him promise that he and Elaine would live in another neighbourhood and, in what they considered would be a proper home.

Eight years later Hyman arranged for him and Elaine to celebrate their anniversary by having dinner at Tony's restaurant. When he was younger and was Tony's most faithful customer Tony had often joked with him about getting married. He would yell from the kitchen that Hyman should meet a young lady from Calabria. They are the best, he said. Failing that he should marry anyone honourable. And he would come dance at his wedding.

Hyman had wanted for many years to present Elaine to Tony. He had even imagined the scene. Tony would come out of the kitchen, approach them both, greet Hyman and gallantly take Elaine's hand. And Hyman would beam proudly as he admired his wife and witnessed this old covenant between friends being fulfilled.

It hadn't happened yet, though, and in fact Hyman had hardly seen Tony in all this time. He and Elaine lived in N.D.G., a fair distance from the old neighbourhood. He worked even further away, in an industrial park in the north end of the city where he was a computer executive for a large manufacturer. He and Elaine tended to spend evenings at home. There was now a small daughter to care for. But tonight it was all arranged. The baby sitter was booked. They were going out.

Tony had by then moved his restaurant to a new location on St. Lawrence Blvd. near Prince Arthur. When they arrived Hyman and Elaine were seated by the head waiter at a small corner table. The restaurant was packed. Cigarette smoke and the low but constant rumble of conversation were suspended in the air.

"When Tony was on Fairmount I would always read the evening paper as I ate," Hyman said shortly after they were seated. "I'd spread it out all over the table. Tony always served me himself. He would put the plates down really carefully, so as not to cover the article I was reading. Some nights were really slow and Tony worked alone as the waiter, cook and dishwasher."

Elaine paused for a moment and looked up from her menu at the crowded restaurant.

"He seems to have done pretty well for himself since then," she said. Then she returned to the menu, her real concern at the moment.

"No, it wouldn't go over very well if I spread out the paper here," said Hyman.

"How about mussels to start with?" asked Elaine.

"Sure, that's fine. I hope he's around," he said, swivelling in his seat, as if searching. "He's probably in the kitchen. You know he never charged me more than three dollars for any meal."

"Yes, I know," said Elaine. "You told me before. Have you

decided what you want?"

They were mid-way through the meal when Tony appeared. He stepped out of the kitchen, wearing his white apron and began walking towards the head waiter at the front of the restaurant. A cigarette dangled from one hand. In the second that he observed him walk Hyman noticed that Tony looked tired, much older, paunchier. Just as he was about to pass he called to him.
"Tony."
Tony stopped and peered over at Hyman, almost squinting as if trying to make out who it was who had called out. Then he approached.
"C'est moi, Tony. Le Professeur."
Tony paused a moment.
"Ah, oui," he said quickly, "comment ça va?"
He quickly shook Hyman's hand and was about to turn to continue on his way when Hyman gestured to Elaine.
"Tony, ma femme."
"Ah, oui," said Tony. "Bonjour." He shook her hand as quickly as he had shook Hyman's. Then he walked away.
Hyman and Elaine went back to their meal. The food was quite good. The bill at the end, wine included, was $35.82.

"That was a good meal," said Elaine as they stepped out of the restaurant into the evening street.
"Would you like to walk for awhile?" he asked.
"I don't know," said Elaine. "I think I'll check in with the sitter about Jessica."
"Everything's fine," he said. "It's only nine o'clock."
"Just the same, I'd like to phone in."
Hyman waited while Elaine walked to a phone booth. He raised one leg and supported himself against a building behind him as he looked out at the street and felt the warm July breeze. Then, suddenly, something came to him. "That's it," he said to himself. He was aware of a sensation that he hadn't felt in a long time. And he knew what it was.
"That's it."
He was feeling the presence of the city, its heat and traffic

71

and exhaustion. And he was sensing the laughing people dressed in their evening clothes, brushing against each other as they passed on the street. It was coming back to him. He hadn't felt the city this way in a long time.

"Everything's fine," said Elaine when she returned. "I told the sitter we'd be home in an hour, though. That gives us half an hour if you like."

They started off along St. Lawrence until Milton, and then along Milton towards the remnants of the student ghetto.

"This used to be my turf when I was a student," Hyman said. "I lived up on Clark because it was a lot cheaper, but I used to hang around here a lot."

"It's all being turned into condominiums now," said Elaine.

"Would you like to buy one?" he asked.

"What?" said Elaine, very surprised.

"Buy one," he repeated. "We could sell the house in N.D.G. and move back downtown."

"You can't be serious," said Elaine. "I thought you liked where we lived."

"It's O.K."

"So why move?"

"It was just a thought."

"Well think about something else. Look around you. You can't bring up kids here. Where would they play? Besides, you don't belong downtown. That's for artists and C.B.C. people."

"Maybe later, when Jessica's grown up."

"A lot later," said Elaine.

They continued walking. He didn't feel put off by their exchange. The evening streets were lovely. He felt light, as if he were floating. Perhaps it was the wine from dinner, the warm breeze, the streets he hadn't seen for a long time. Then, suddenly, a shudder ran through him. It was imperceptible to Elaine but he felt it well through his body. He recognized it. It was the same shudder he had felt when he first slept with Elaine and again when his daughter was born. And then he remembered when he had first felt it. It was two months after he had left his family and was living alone. At that time he was also walking down an evening street, perhaps this same one. Suddenly he felt it. He had survived. He was managing alone. And there was hope for more, even better things. There was wonder in this world. He was part of an adventure.

"You know Jessica wants to take water ballet classes," said Elaine.

"Huh?" answered Hyman.

"Didn't you hear what I said?" asked Elaine crossly. "Where are you tonight?"

"I'm sorry. What was it about Jessica?"

"She wants to take water ballet. They teach it at the Y."

"So enroll her."

"Don't you think she's too young?"

"If the Y says it's O.K. then it's O.K. They have instructors. They know what they're doing."

"I suppose you're right. I shouldn't worry about her so much. I just look at her sometimes and she looks. . .so small."

"She's almost seven years old. There's nothing fragile about her."

"You're right," she sighed.

She was quiet for a moment, then continued.

"There's something else we have to talk about. Her school for next year. We have to decide if it's going to be regular French school or French immersion."

"Is there a deadline?"

"Soon, in a few weeks."

"We'll decide in time," he said, without looking at her. It was as if he wasn't speaking to her at all.

Elaine was about to pounce on him but decided to hold off. Let him dream, she thought. They continued walking slowly, silently. He took her hand.

Then he stopped.

"It's still there," he said.

"What is?" asked Elaine.

"That little restaurant. Do you see?"

He pointed across the street to a snack bar so small it couldn't hold more than eight people.

"It looks almost the same as it did then," he continued.

"That's where I spent my eighteenth birthday."

"It doesn't look a very cheerful place for a celebration," she said.

"No, it wasn't."

He paused, still looking at it.

"I wonder if the two guys still work there."

"Which guys?" she asked. Her patience was being tried.

"The two big fat ones that worked there. Or maybe just one of them worked there and the other was his friend. I never figured it out. Would you like to hear about it?"

"Is it a long story?"

"Not too long," he answered. "You see, it all started in the McGill library. This was before I had rented the room on Clark and I was still living with my parents. Or rather, I slept there. I really lived in the library, like a lot of other students. We were a little community, the regulars on the floor, and we knew each other well, if only by sight.

"Anyway, I finished studying one evening around nine and happened to leave at the same time as another student. Her name was Linda and although I had never spoken to her I had seen her many times. She was tall and blonde and wore tiny, oval-rimmed glasses. She was two years ahead of me and I remember her looking much older and more mature than me. She was really a woman. At that time I still felt pretty much like a boy.

"We took the same elevator down and began talking. She noticed I was carrying several reference books on Chaucer. She had done a paper on him the year before and asked how my work was going. Like many older students she was trying to be helpful. When we left the library we discovered we were both walking to the number eighty bus on Jeanne Mance and we kept talking as we walked along Milton. Somewhere in the conversation I mentioned that it was my eighteenth birthday. It really was. I just didn't feel like there was much to celebrate. But she got all excited, as if this was a big event in my life and it was imperative that it be noted in some way. We were standing across the street from the snack bar and she said, 'At least let me buy you a cup of coffee.' I resisted a bit, not wanting to make a fuss, and said it wasn't necessary. But she insisted and I went along. There were only two people in the restaurant at that time, a couple of big, stout men. One was behind the counter. The other was sitting on a stool. They were talking softly. It looked like this was a quiet moment they shared before they shut down for the night. We sat at the one small table they had and Linda ordered two cups of coffee. The man behind the counter, he looked to be in his forties, seemed surprised that two customers were coming in at this time, but he served us and then went back to his friend. His friend had an eye on us as we drank and asked 'You are students?' I said yes and he asked what we studied. I answered 'literature', for both of us. 'Ah, literature,' he said. 'That is a beautiful subject. Very beautiful.'

"Linda and I drank our coffee. We talked a bit about school. And she quizzed me about my birthday, saying things like, 'Hey, you should celebrate. This is a big day. Eighteen is a very romantic age. That's when everybody falls in love.'

"As soon as we finished our coffees the man behind the counter approached and took our cups away. It was time for him to close down. But he was nice about it, and smiled as he cleared the table. I was about to pay but he brushed me off saying, 'No, no. Not necessary.' Then he started turning off the lights.

"We all left together and just as we exited he said to both of us, 'Come, I will drive you home.' I said we could take the bus but he insisted and led us to his large Ford. Linda and I sat in the back and he and his friend in front. Occasionally his friend turned to us and said things like, 'To be a student is a wonderful thing,' and 'The young people, they will save us.' "

"Weren't you afraid, going off with a couple of strangers?" interrupted Elaine.

"Not at that time," said Hyman. "When you're young, you're very trusting. At least I was.

"After driving for about ten minutes," he continued, "they pulled over on a quiet street. The talkative friend took out a hash pipe, lit it and passed it around in the car. Then he started singing in Greek. He sang beautifully, with great passion. He stopped for a moment to explain that he was singing political songs that had been banned by the Colonels. He said that really they were about love. By then Linda and I were stoned. We were giggling and laughing and humming along with his songs. Then Linda an-

75

nounced that today was my birthday. Our singer got excited. He reached over and shook my hand. Then he put his hand in his pocket, took out a ten dollar bill and offered it to me. I refused but he practically shoved it into my hand. 'Please, it is a present,' he said. 'You are the hope of the world.'

"After half an hour they started driving again. The singer continued his songs, but with a much lower voice. His songs sounded sadder now, almost plaintive. In the back seat Linda moved closer to me and slowly put her hand in mine.

"They arrived at my house first. I would have been happy to stay in that car and drive forever. But I couldn't. This was home. Back to ground zero. After I left the car I paused for a moment. In the instant before they drove off Linda and I looked at each other through the window of the back door. She looked beautiful, sad. Then I saw a tear and realized she was crying. I wanted so much to reach out and touch her but the car was already moving.

"I saw Linda two days later on our floor in the library. She laughed about our experience and those 'two funny men.' I asked if anything had happened after they drove off and she said, 'No, we just talked a bit in the car.' We both paused, as if there was more to be said about them, about her. But she forced a smile and, trying to return to her former cheer said, 'They were really nice and let me off at my door.'

"I saw her a couple of more times in the library but both times she was in the company of a graduate student, probably her boyfriend. They seemed preoccupied with each other. I didn't want to intrude and we just nodded in passing. Then she graduated and that was it. Everybody goes their own way. I hope she's well."

He paused and looked for a moment at the restaurant.

"That was my eighteenth birthday," he said.

"I hope your other birthdays are just as interesting," answered Elaine. "We'd better go now. I promised the sitter we'd be home by ten."

Jessica was sound asleep when they returned home. There had been no problems and the sitter had spent the evening watching television.

Hyman and Elaine went to bed at ten-thirty. Elaine fell sound asleep almost immediately but Hyman remained awake. He stared at the ceiling for awhile and then slowly removed himself to that indistinct space between sleep and waking. "Hope." The word drifted to him. "Hope," he thought again in this half wakefulness. "This thing called hope can be put together in such a way. And Tony, he had hope for everything that was. And now there was a restaurant full of well-dressed people, and even if Tony no longer remembered the poor student he had served in a past time success of one sort had been attained. And the songs of revolution and smoky intoxication in the rear of an automobile. There was hope there too. And even in a crowded room, and in Chaucer, and in a library where there was a girl with oval glasses."

And then he started and rose with force.

"Elaine!" he said almost violently as he reached over and shook her awake. "Elaine, I have to speak to you. We should have more children. We should. And that condominium downtown. It's possible. We could do it."

"Hyman," she said, angry at being woken. "Your eighteenth birthday was a long time ago, O.K.? I love you but, please, just go to sleep." She returned to her pillow, burying herself in it as if to shut out another's dreams.

Hyman lay back and in a moment returned to this semi-awake state that served as a conduit for his prayers. "And for sleep there is hope too," he thought. "Yes, and there are dreams that don't die in the morning but that well through the body like a shudder on a vacant street. And sleep really is just a respite between dreams, for all is possible and there really are realms of adventure. Perhaps," he thought. "Of course," he answered. "Of course there is no fear. And I have no fear. The day will always be brave. And sleep...and sleep will always welcome our night."

Lament for a Son

AFTER MY FATHER broke his back he spent most of his time in an easy chair, reading the afternoon papers and looking out the window. I think that he looked on his convalescence as something of a long vacation, one that might possibly never end. Twenty-two years of driving a cab had been plenty to him and he was now in no hurry to return to work. His accident had happened one morning at two-thirty when a drunk plowed into his car. He had spent three months in a cast in the hospital and was now spending nine months resting at home. That was all he had to show for twenty-two years of service to his company.

Despite his infirmity he still appeared quite handsome and in good physical shape—that is when his shirt wasn't open so that the bars and clamps of his back brace were visible. Unlike many cab drivers who became overweight over the years, he had remained slim and he still had a full head of hair, although it had now almost completely greyed. He wasn't a bad looking man. He was also the most uncomplaining person I had ever known.

My father had not had an easy life and had not lived up to, what I would consider, his true potential. Although he had completed high school, he had never been able to go to university or to continue studying the classical clarinet which had been his main ambition. Nor had he been a success in the business ventures he attempted. His most major attempt to be an entrepeneur failed miserably. He opened a clothing factory with a partner. The partner cheated him, the factory went bankrupt. My father returned to driving a cab. He was too trusting to believe anyone could take advantage of him and later too timid to demand restitution. He refused to hurt other people. These same people took advantage of his weakness to hurt him. So we remained poor, my

78

father drove a cab, and now he spent most of his days sitting in an easy chair and looking out the window. Still, he never complained. He never indulged in self-pity or demanded any special attention for himself. I saw in him a certain dignity—that of someone who had done his best and never cheated anyone, and I admired him more than any person in the world.

It saddened him to see me unemployed and even more to see me idling about the house, doing nothing in particular. I often found myself sitting in a chair near him, perhaps also looking out the window. My routine was certainly not very exciting. Three cups of coffee spread out at intervals over the morning, lunch at Tony's restaurant down the street, the afternoon paper, perhaps a few beers at Wilson's Tavern. Most evenings I watched television or occasionally went to a film.

The tavern was a form of refuge for me in the afternoons. It was a dimly lit, smoke-filled environment that, being a Quebec tavern, only admitted men. Silent men sat at tables in the afternoons drinking draft beer quietly. Many were unshaved and wore clothes imbued with weeks of city dirt. But at the tavern they could sit in peace, secure in this brotherhood of silence and forgetfullness, protected from whatever difficulties that existed for them outside the saloon doors. The tavern was their sanctuary and I suppose it was mine also. I could sit there in seclusion, alone at a table, read the afternoon paper and slowly drink the beer which I had come to know as the best source, or relief, for aloneness.

At home I was always conscious of the telephone. Although very few calls were actually for me—they were mostly from friends and relatives of my parents inquiring about my father's health—I still started each time I heard a ringing. I was trying to succeed as a film editor in the motion picture industry and the whole process of waiting and anticipating jobs had put me on edge. And of course my choice of occupation, or usually nonexistent occupation, was a source of conflict between myself and my parents.

My father and I occasionally made idle conversation about politics, literature, (for he was a fairly well-read man), the cab business, even the weather on particularly empty days. Occasionally he would talk about his young days studying clarinet in Europe and his adventures as a young immigrant. These reminiscences were always the best part of any conversation. I enjoyed hearing him talk about the days when he was young and poor but certainly not without ambition. I could see that he enjoyed recounting these tales. Although he did not become any more animated, the faint smiles that came to his lips indicated that these recollections gave him a form of inner pleasure. He was thinking back to the days when he was younger, stronger and full of hope. Unfortunately, any extended conversation always deteriorated into the same dreary conflict.

"You don't want to drive a cab?"

"No, Pop, I don't want to."

"It isn't so bad, you know. I did it for over twenty years. You could make some money on top of the unemployment insurance."

"I'm not interested in earning extra money that way. Besides, I have enough to live on."

"So why don't you seriously consider going back to school. Or at least take some courses. I know you don't want to be a lawyer or go into business but you could take a masters degree. You always liked reading. An M.A. in English can always come in useful. You could teach afterwards, get a job in a college. What's the use of waiting around for your big film producers to call? Editing films is nice work if you can do it regularly, but there's no point in being unemployed two-thirds of the year. An intelligent boy like you sitting around the house. With your knowledge and skills you could be making something of yourself—earning a good living."

I could feel my impatience with his words welling up in me. But I knew I would have to restrain myself. I cared for my father too much to be vocally angry. My replies to him were more in the form of pleas than arguments.

"Look, Pop, I like working with film. I like it even when I'm not doing it. I have to give it a chance or I'll never know if I could make it. Don't you understand? It all takes time. Besides, I'm only twenty-four. It's not the end."

"Sure, sure, I understand. But my opinion, and I'm not saying this just to make you angry, is that you're selling yourself short. Look at me. I could have been an accomplished musician if

I had continued studying. I could be playing with the Montreal Symphony and earning, maybe, four hundred dollars a week instead of spending half my life working in a cab."

He paused to make himself more comfortable in his back brace, then turned to me again.

"All right, when I was your age the Depression was on and there were no opportunities for a boy like me so I had to work and give up studying. But you have all the opportunities. And don't worry about money. I'll loan you money to go back to school."

"I don't want any of your money, you know that."

"Are you sure? It's there, for you. I don't need it."

"Look, how many times do we have to discuss this? I'm doing what I want to do. It takes time, that's all. Besides, there may be a big job coming up. Hector is trying to produce a feature and if it comes off he wants me to edit it. It'll be a good job with lots of money."

"Sure, more promises. You still have faith in these people?"

"Look, there's no point talking about this any more." My impatience had risen to the inevitable frustration. I rose and walked to the window. Then I turned around. My father was staring silently. All I could say was, "You want a cup of tea?"

"No thanks," he replied. "I just want to read the paper."

"Good enough," I said. "I'm going out for a walk."

My mother worked shifts as a telephone receptionist in a hospital. Like my father she had still managed to remain slim and although her hair had turned completely white at forty, she still was, in her own way, attractive. My uncles used to tell me that as a young lady she was a true beauty, much admired and sought after by suitors. But she had been an orphan—her parents died when she was six years old in a typhoid epidemic in Poland—and, as they say, she had had none of the advantages. She had little education and had been forced to start working in sweat shop factories at the age of fifteen. But she was constantly trying to improve herself. She would cut articles out of newspapers to save in a box and re-read. Occasionally she would attempt to read a biography of some famous person whom she considered inspirational, meaning someone who was self made and successful, although she read so slowly that it might take her six months to get through one hundred pages. And she took night classes in French grammar at the local high school.

She worked diligently at her job and zealously at maintaining a scrupulously tidy house. She considered her whole life a sacrifice for the welfare of her family. Whatever money she had left over after expenses she saved assiduously in the bank, often stating that it would be her legacy to me. I told her that I did not want any of her money and that she should not talk foolishly about distant matters such as death. She would just shrug and I would not pursue the matter for fear of starting an argument. Still, the arguments did come. Her nagging, (at least that is how I interpreted her interest in my welfare) became unbearable. Any conversation longer than a minute inevitably led into a variation of the same conflicts.

"Clara called you last night."

"Thanks for the message."

"Are you going to call her back?"

"Yes."

"When?"

"I don't know when. When I feel like talking to her. Anyways, it's none of your business."

"It is my business. You're my son and I care about you. I want to see you happy, married, with a proper home. I don't want you to become an old bachelor, all alone."

"Listen, I'll manage fine, all right. I can take care of my own life."

"Look, why don't you call Clara? She's a pleasant girl. She has a good teaching job, owns a car. She's not bad looking, you know. Don't you like her?"

"Yes, I like her well enough."

"So why don't you think about settling down?"

"Listen ma, I don't go around prying into your life and telling you who you should be friends with. So do me a favour and leave me alone. If I want to call Clara I'll call her and that's all you have to know."

"I love you, Simon. Please don't hurt me. You're my son."

"Oh, for Christ's sake. I don't want to hurt you. I don't want to hurt anyone. All I want is to be left alone to live my life in peace. Will you begrudge me that?"

My mother let out a low sigh. She rested her hands on a kitchen counter and was still for a few seconds. Then she began taking some pots out of a cupboard.

"What do you want for supper tonight?"

"Anything, anything at all."

"Is fish all right?"

It was my turn to be silent. My fingers made a circular pattern on the tablecloth. Then I looked up.

"Sure, fish is fine."

When the phone rang I was sitting in an old captain's chair with a book in my lap. It was 11:30 in the morning and I had read four pages in two hours. My father answered the phone and stretching in his back brace handed me the receiver.

"Hello, Simon. It's Hector."

"Oh yeah. What's up?"

"Nothing much yet. No news about the feature. Schwartz and his accountants are still trying to make up their minds about the financing. But don't worry, you'll be the first to know. Listen, I'm here at the lab and I met a guy named Fred Silver who's just finishing off a film and says he needs an editor for a few days. I don't know very much about it but the film is a porno feature. I've seen a bit of it and to tell the truth it doesn't look very good. Anyways, if you're interested in a few days work I can call him to the phone to talk with you. You want me to call him?"

I felt hesitant but nevertheless said that I would speak to him.

I waited on the phone about two minutes. I heard distant footsteps, then the sounds of someone approaching the phone and then the connection.

"Hello, you Simon Miller?" The voice sounded fast and impatient.

"That's me."

"Well, listen. How good are you?"

83

The question made me uneasy, partly because of its abruptness and partly because I felt I had not as yet been given the opportunity to really prove myself, at least to my satisfaction.

"If you want I could give you a list of my credits," I replied.

"O.K., but quickly."

I mentioned the major 35mm. films I had worked on as an assistant editor and the smaller 16mm. films that I had edited by myself or with the director.

Silver spoke again: "Well, listen. What I have here is a 16mm. feature. The picture editing is finished. Now what I want is an outside editor who's got a good eye to sit down with it for a couple of days and clean it up. You think you can do that?"

"What do you mean by clean it up?"

"You know. Trim it a bit. Make sure the cuts match. Speed up the rhythm. I'm going to be in my editing room in Cine-Tel this afternoon at two. If you're interested come by and we'll talk. Bye."

The phone came down abruptly on the other end. I hung up more slowly, holding the dead receiver in my hand for several seconds.

"Who was that?" my father asked.

"Oh, some director who needs some work done on a film. I may get a job for a couple of days."

"No word from any of your big producers?"

"No, Dad, no word yet."

I found Silver sitting in an editing room in Cine-Tel, a company that rented out editing facilities. Except for a large editing machine and three chairs the room was bare. Silver was sitting in a chair talking to a handsome, blond-haired young man who was leaning against the machine. Sitting in a corner of the room and looking on nonchalantly was an equally blonde-haired young lady. Both were tanned and both looked like they had just come out of a California surfing film. Silver looked about thirty. His face was covered with a half grown beard and he was wearing knee-high leather boots, leather pants and a leather vest over a red and white striped shirt. He looked up and saw me standing by the door.

"You Miller?" he said.

I nodded.

"I'm Fred Silver. This is an actor from the film," he said gesturing to the young man standing next to him. "We're going to be looking at a few scenes. You can watch and tell me if you're interested in spending a few days on it. It's a gay porno, by the way. It's being made for the New York market."

The blond young man put out the lights and Silver turned on the editing machine. The first scene on the roll was of two men getting out of a cab. One was arguing with the driver about the fare. It cut to the two men drinking cocktails in an apartment. That cut to a bedroom scene. One man was lying nude on a bed. The other was giving him a blow job. The camera did not move. The scene was taken from one angle, in mid-shot. It must have lasted for over five minutes but that is only an estimate because I walked out of the room before the shot was over.

Silver found me talking to Ginette, the receptionist. She was a friendly person and was telling me the latest film industry gossip.

Silver spoke first. He didn't seem to mind that I had walked out before the end of the roll.

"So, what did you think?"

"It's pretty static."

"Sure it's static. What did you expect, an art film? The whole thing cost less than thirty thousand dollars. Shot in in ten days. I wasn't aiming for any masterpiece. So listen, are you interested in cleaning it up?"

"What can you pay?"

"Seventy-five dollars a day. Shouldn't take you more than three days. You interested?"

"I'll think about it," I replied.

"Sure, you do that. Adios," he said as he raised his hand to me and walked out towards the washroom in the hallway. Our whole exchange had not lasted more than a minute.

I looked at Ginette. She looked at me with eyes that seemed sympathetic. She shrugged. I said good-bye and left, hoping that I would not see Silver coming out of the washroom.

I never did call Silver. And it was a long time before I called Clara. That night I went to Wilson's Tavern. I sat alone at a table and read the evening edition of the *Montreal Star*, slowly drinking my two draft beer.

At a nearby table Jimmy, a regular, was regaling his wino buddies with loud stories. He had been crippled in an industrial accident many years before and now walked with two canes. He was telling his friends about his accident and subsequent stays in hospital. I listened to his stories for awhile. Then I went back to reading the paper.

When I got home I found my father leaning back in his chair by the window. His eyes were closed, the evening paper lay spread out on his lap, ready to fall off any moment. I stood in the doorway looking at him, at the worn oriental rug on the floor, the photograph of him as a young man dressed in a fine suit, holding a clarinet, the wedding photograph of him and my mother on the mantlepiece, the old books lining the walls, the plants that had not grown any larger in fifteen years. I stood there and inhaled the musty odour of the house that had been lived in too long, where a young man had no business being. And then I walked over to where my father sat and I placed my hand on his. His flesh was smooth on the outside but calloused on the inside from the years of holding a steering wheel. As I touched him he opened his eyes and slightly turned his head to look at me. "Everything's going to be all right, Dad," I said. "Don't worry, everything's going to be all right." He opened his eyes a bit more. I could not tell what he was trying to say but it seemed—I hoped—they were saying, "I know son, I know." Then he turned his head away, slowly closing his eyes. And I stood there, lightly holding his hand, wishing there was something else I could say.

Simon Goes to London

WHEN HE WAS TWENTY-ONE he left Montreal and went to the art school in London. He left the city of spiral staircases and iron balconies and snow and frost that clung to the trees and found himself in a room in the north of London. There, instead of hearing French and Portuguese, Greek, Italian and English in the streets, all he heard was a British English that seemed cold and distant. And instead of "Monsieur" or "Sir" he became "Guv" or "Squire" and sometimes, "Lad." The ladies in the local shops often called him "Love" or "Dear." At first these appellations seemed strange and contradictory. There were terms of endearment, and yet the people were certainly not dear to him. Still, he became accustomed to them and even enjoyed hearing himself addressed in such ways. He was, after all, alone much of the time and although he knew that these terms were not intended in any serious or literal way, being addressed by them gave him the feeling that he was somehow a wanted and accepted part of this new world.

He was the only lodger in the house in Muswell Hill where he let his room. Mrs. Grady, the proprietor, was a widow. She had not intended to rent out any of her rooms after her husband's death, but found that it was necessary in order to supplement her pension. But she was happy with her tenant. Such a quiet boy, she thought. Sometimes they would watch television together in the sitting room.

He cooked his meals on a hotplate in his room. He had a small radio, a soft double bed, an old floral pattern rug, one chair, a small table and a wardrobe. The walls were covered with a wallpaper patterned with swans drifting in a lake against a forest background. Because of age it now had a grey veil over it, as did all the wallpaper in the house. The wallpaper made him slightly uneasy. It spoke to him too much of empty and sad times. Behind it he saw a history of bombing raids and blackouts, wages of eleven pounds a week and two weeks vacation at Blackpool, bitter typhoo tea, grey skies and coal burning in the fireplace vainly attempting to generate warmth. These were memories that he was aware of but were nevertheless foreign to him. They were memories of Mrs. Grady and the millions like her and he wanted no part of them. He hated the memories and felt sorry for the people.

In his room he also kept his sketch pads, and pencils, some oil paints, canvas and his few books. Every morning he would walk a mile-and-a-half to the art school in the Alexandra Palace on a hill overlooking London. The walk took him past row houses, each with its small garden, past the shops and then through the park that led up to the Palace. There he would pass the small duck pond and gazebo, the ladies with their prams and the workmen raking leaves off the ground. So often there was a mist hanging in the air. In the autumn he could smell the leaves being burned and see the grey smoke suspended in the mist and blending with it.

The studio at the college was a very large room that had once been an indoor gymnasium. Twenty foot high windows lined one side of it giving a view of the park and letting in pleasing daylight. The room was empty at first but it did not remain that way for very long. In the first weeks of the term all the students constructed dividers out of plywood which they used to seal themselves off with their work. Simon also built his enclosure and became almost invisible in this labyrinth mass. It was here that he painted and sketched and occasionally read his books. He had a small hotplate on his drawing table and often he would boil water and brew a cup of black tea. While he drank it he would sit on his small stool covered with multicoloured paint and look through a book, or at his paintings. Sometimes he would just sit in silence.

Every afternoon he would eat lunch at the school cafeteria. It was a small room that could only hold about forty people at a time. The menu consisted mostly of cornish pasties or steak and kidney pies, warmed over in an old gas oven and served with watery brown gravy. This was new food to him. At first he

88

enjoyed trying this new type of cooking. But soon the novelty wore off. The food was not very good but it was all there was. The other students did not seem to mind. Lunch was the only time they could escape from the echoes of the studio and sit as a group without plywood barriers.

He would eat his meals almost stoically for the food became less and less appetizing as the year progressed. Like the wallpaper the food was part of this new environment that he could tolerate and live with, but never accept, never be a part of. And as usual he would wash his meal down with black tea. And as usual he sat alone.

But this aloneness could not persist. And as he sat in his room or in the cafeteria or in his plywood cubicle he knew that someone would eventually break through this world of his. And when she sat down opposite him one lunch hour at the cafeteria he lifted his head to look at her before they both awkwardly turned away, nervously grasping cups of hot tea. But he knew that someone had made the first step at entering, and perhaps sharing, his world.

She was twenty-two years old with long blond hair that ballooned out and fell almost to her waist. She had a full flushed face and her cheeks were always red, as though she had just come in from the cold. There was an enquiring, full look to her. And she was beautiful.

They sat opposite each other alone at the table for several minutes in silence as they drank their tea. And then he said, "My name's Simon."

"I'm Caroline," she replied in a low voice. She smiled slightly as she said it and they looked at each other's faces for a moment before their gazes dropped again to the table. It was a long, awkward minute but already he could feel this invisible bond between them. Then she rose, saying she had to work, and left. A few seconds later he also got up, put his mug back on the counter, and returned to his plywood cubicle in the studio.

At five that evening he walked through the maze of barriers in the studio looking for her. He found her sitting in a small enclosure looking at some watercolours she had completed. He asked her if she would like to come to his house, to perhaps drink some wine.

For the next six weeks she would walk home with him, every third or fourth evening. They would sit in his room, he on his bed, she in the large overstuffed armchair. She often sat wearing her large Afghan coat. Most often he would talk about Montreal. She would accuse him of being homesick and he would laugh, knowing he had no defence. Nevertheless, he would continue to talk about the city he knew, about the snow and cold and the spring when everything was renewed and people would smile again as they walked in the streets. He talked about the neighbourhoods where he had lived, where many different languages were spoken and described the smells of the shops and restaurants where one could find paella, gnocchi, polish sausages, blintzes, souvlaki. And he described the houses with balconies and spiral staircases and the outside steps that he spent many summer days sitting on, waving to friends who passed by, watching the activity in the street. He remarked that he was saddened to see that nobody appeared to sit outside their homes in London, that everybody seemed to lock themselves inside behind oak doors and grey stone walls.

She never talked very much about herself. She was with him and he felt that was enough. He was afraid that prying into her would destroy it all. Often they would sip wine and listen to his second-hand records on his small phonograph. Sometimes they would go to a pub in the evenings and drink ginger wine. At ten pence it was the least expensive drink in the pubs but the syrupy liquid warmed them on the clammy, damp nights. They grew to be comfortable with each other. And every evening around ten she would say, "I must go," and would leave him to his empty room. Sometimes Mrs. Grady would peek out of the front parlour as she left, but she never said anything about her visits.

It happened after six weeks. It was April now and just as their original meeting was inevitable, so was this encounter. Nothing came easily to him. Nothing fit together just right.

It was in the late evening and they were in his room sipping ginger wine. He had purchased a bottle several weeks ago just for these moments when they were alone. At ten she said, "I must

90

go." And for the first time, instead of silently seeing her leave, he interrupted her. Taking hold of her hand he said, "Please don't." And she looked back at him with a look that mirrored his own. It was a sad look, a longing look.

"You know I'm married, don't you?" she said.

When he looked surprised she said quietly, "I thought everyone knew I was married. My husband lives in Brighton. He's a student at the University of Sussex. We have a flat in Kent where we live during the summers. I thought you knew all that." And he replied in his own low voice, "No, I didn't know. I don't talk to very many people at the college. There wasn't really any way I could know."

Then there was a moment of silence, like a punctuation mark that was separating everything that came before and everything that would happen from now on. He was looking at her but her head was bowed. They were both seeing the past six weeks pass before them, as they sat there together.

Then he said, "You don't have to go, you know." There was another pause, before she replied in a low voice, uttered as if she was in reality only speaking to herself, "No, I suppose I don't."

And so she returned to him and to their wallpapered room and coal fire and double bed with a sagging mattress, and to the blues records on the small gramophone. And the next morning and many mornings afterwards they would wake up at eight and take a bottle of milk off the windowsill and make two cups of tea. They would sit by the tiny table drinking their morning tea, and eating breakfast. They grew to be comfortable in their North London bedsitter and would often exchange glances and smiles, unaccompanied by words, but which nevertheless spoke the love that grew between them.

At the end of May her husband completed school in Brighton. He took a flat in London and Caroline went to join him. She disappeared silently, as silently as she had met him. One evening she did not walk through the vestibule beyond Mrs. Grady's front door and enter Simon's second floor room. When he saw her in school several days later they sat together for a few moments in the cafeteria and she told him that she would stay with her husband now that he was in London and that she did not know when she could see her young Canadian. She would not even be at the Palace because she had work to do at another campus of the college.

Their encounter was brief, only a few moments. It was awkward. And Simon was left alone again, unsure, bewildered. He felt a great sense of loss which soon began to channel itself into restless wanderings. He would often go for long walks by himself through Highgate Wood and the evening streets of his own neighbourhood. Once, on a long walk through the wood he decided to continue on to Hampstead Heath and Hampstead Village where he stopped in to eat at a pub and had three pints of stout. A fitting thing to do, he thought, for a wounded heart. At the third pint, in his reverie, he found himself wishing he was Irish. In his romantic vision he thought that somehow if he were Irish it would be more legitimate for him to cry. Too bad I'm not in Dublin, he thought. I could crawl from pub to pub with my mates. They would curse women and help me forget. We could stand on O'Connel Bridge, under the stars, and shout harsh words to the air as the Liffy flowed beneath us. That would be grand. To channel anger into poetry. Perhaps that would help me forget.

But of course that was just a dream and in reality he missed her deeply. Sometimes he would try to rationalize the matter. Someone had thought highly enough of him to offer him their love, to devote themselves to him. Wasn't that enough? But unfortunately such matters do not lend themselves to that kind of logic and the pain was just as strong as before. He wished he could contact her but no one had phones and London was so confusing he was afraid of losing his way if he attempted to go to the flat where she now lived. And even if he did make the journey, what would he say if it was her husband who answered the door? So he tried to divert himself instead. He worked hard at his art, continued his long walks, drank warm beer in pubs, watched television with Mrs. Grady.

Finally, at the end of the school year he did arrange to meet her. He left notes for her at the school and they agreed to see each other outside the Palace on the last day of classes. The weather had by then turned warm and the sun shone almost every day. His spirits were now better. As in Montreal, the spring brought smiles back to people.

They sat on the grass, on a lower slope below the Palace. There were other students sitting on a higher slope above them, lolling about on the huge lawn, chatting among themselves or just lying back, taking in the day's warmth. It was summer, a time to escape from the constricting plywood cubicles.

Neither Simon nor Caroline said very much. They sat on the lawn, their eyes half closed because of the brightness. In a way there was not much to say. He knew this would probably be the last time he would see her. But much of the sense of loss he felt before had by then been relieved. Instead, he was beginning to realize the feeling of liberation that often comes with the irrevocable end of an affair of love.

When they did speak it was mostly about his future. He said that he would soon be going back to Montreal, to pick up where he had left off. He would find a place to live and if possible, a studio. He would be an artist. It would be difficult at first, and probably for a long time after, but he felt comfortable with his choice because it was like an adventure and there would always be something new to look forward to. His art would grow as he grew and the real adventure lay in never knowing exactly which direction this whole process would take. And there was also the city itself to look forward to. This North London had never been his home. Now he would return to his real home, his friends, and the familiar streets he felt so comfortable on.

Caroline smiled at him. He noticed how the sun caught her blond hair. He wanted to kiss her but he hesitated. He was aware of the other students sitting above them. They had kept their love a secret and he had always been very discreet in order to protect her. But today was different. It was the end, but also a beginning. The coming of summer somehow indicated a new order of things. He leaned over and kissed her on her lips and she smiled again. They both sat without speaking for another minute and then she leaned over, and still smiling returned his kiss. Then she rose and walked down the slope to the W3 bus which would take her back to London.

He watched her disappear down the slope. Then he lay back in the grass, feeling the heat of the day on his pale skin. Yes, he would return to his home. But first he knew what he would do. He would go to Ireland. There he would find a farm in County Clare to work on. He would walk in the mists and look at the sea and listen to the fiddles and pipes. That was where he belonged now, close to the rich earth and to kind people. He was sure he would feel close to them. He would find his song.

He lay back on the grass and closed his eyes. He felt much better. The sun had put his mind at ease.